I0690465

Career
Criminal
2

Hope you Enjoy,

D. Henderson

Follow D. Henderson
Instagram: @d.henderson3488
Facebook: Darren J. Henderson

Library of Congress Cataloging-in-
Publication Data

Register: 1-6865475321

Copyrights 2018

Cover Design by: Mr. Najji Wells

All rights reserved, including the right to reproduce this
or portions thereof in any form whatsoever.

The Saga Continue
<u>Chapter 1</u>

The physical pain was mild in comparison to the hurt I felt inside my heart. Two months later it was still hard to believe Tanya and my unborn child lost their lives on account of my inability to protect them from the evils of this world. I've never been one to advocate striking the innocent in retaliation for the ills of their loved ones, but I now realized that school of thought was not only out dated, it was a suitable weapon in eliminating any and all future threats. Doc had opened a door I vowed to make him regret. I didn't want him dead, at least not right now; I wanted to kill everyone near and dear in his life. I wanted him to experience the pain I felt a thousand times over before I ended his life.

The Crime Game wasn't the type of profession that provided sick-leave, or compensated for injuries. The road to recovery was painstaking, but like most difficult challenges I embraced the ordeal wholehearted and aggressive. Unable to meet the demands associated with the crime game I went into seclusion, spending the majority of my time in Berkeley, under the care of Trisha, who once again became my anchor in my weakest time.

Suffering from multiple bullet wounds, Trisha enlisted the help of Carrie, whom happened to be her best friend and a physical therapist. Through her guidance, and a great deal of pain I was back on my feet in less than a month. My absence from the hood created a wide range of speculation. Unable to stop or control the flow of rumors I decided to feed into them. Instead of downplaying my injuries I embellished them. The streets didn't give a fuck how you got your issue, whether it was by design, or by accident; there was something very intriguing about the fall of a giant, not only did it make for good gossip, it also revealed hidden haters.

Lil Bull and I had just concluded a series of chess games, in which he won none, when Trisha returned home bright-eyed and smiling as she had every day since my arrival. I greeted her by lifting her from her feet and showering her with kisses from her forehead to her lips. It wasn't until I lowered her and she observed my bags that her body became tense and sadness overcame her.

"You're leaving?" She asked, unable to control the flow of tears coming from her eyes.

"Yes love; it's time for me to go. Don't be sad, I'll be back sooner than you think." I lied.

"Floyd." I placed a finger to her lips. "Please don't make this any harder." I said and kissed her once again. After lowering her head she looked up and smiled. "You must be Kenny." She turned towards Lil Bull and extended her hand.

"Yes I am." Lil Bull smiled, ignored her hand and gave her a hug. "It's a pleasure to finally meet you Trisha."

The afternoon was filled with an abundance of laughter. Lil Bull and Trisha hit it off like they had known each other their entire lives. I was happy he was here to break the ice, I couldn't recall one time I ever handed him the ball and he fumbled. At the first sign of darkness I pulled Trisha to the side to say our farewells. This time she accepted my departure with a smile and a series of kisses.

Lil Bull was waiting outside in a brand new 1987 Range Rover; no sooner than I entered the passenger compartment he handed me a fully loaded 9mm, which I gladly accepted. Unlike our previous encounter I didn't need a pep-talk on the importance of being armed at all times, it went without saying. Unbeknownst to Lil Bull I was no longer a man driven by unrealistic principles and values; the type of values that were more suitable for a law abiding citizen rather than a gangster. The Crime Game was a sport for the wicked, devious, and the deadly; anything less a gangster was asking to come up short.

I felt a slight pain in my torso when I lowered my seat, which was a clear indication I wasn't completely healed. Despite a few aches and pain, mentally I felt a thousand percent prepared for whatever the wicked streets of southeast had in store for me. While most gangsters emerged from a life-threatening ordeal with a change of heart, and ready to hang it up; I on the other hand emerged with a Take no hostage/Take no chances attitude. I was returning with a whole list of unfinished business that had to be addressed immediately. There was nothing more important than avenging the death of my son. Had Doc known the fury that would follow murdering my loved ones, I'm sure he would have thought long and hard before he injected family into our business.

Returning from the dead I felt relieved, like a huge burden had been removed from my heart. I've always known the mentality a gangster must have to survive amongst the demons of this world. A gangster with a conscious was like a shark with no teeth; it was just a matter of time before you became a victim. Never in my life have I ever felt such an overwhelming desire to kill, or questioned the actions of The Almighty. I've always understood the powers of God, His blessings as well as his wrath. What I never understood was His willingness to allow the innocent to suffer and the wicked to flourish.

"What's on your mind?" Lil Bull asked as we hit Interstate 5 heading south.

"I got so much shit floating in the air right now, I feel like there's not enough hours in a day to take care of everything that needs to be handled."

"What's on top of the list?"

"You already know, Doc. Cuz there's not a second that pass I don't think about Doc. I've killed that motha fucka a thousand times in my sleep; and each time has been different. I tell you what I really want; I want his ass to suffer, kill everybody he ever loved, than skin his ass alive." Caught up in the moment I hadn't realized a salvage pleasure had appeared on my face. Lil Bull glanced at me briefly, witnessing the beast within, the monster that even the hardest gangsters would come to fear.

Prior to killing Zuberi I thought long and hard of the ramifications. Regardless of his imperfections I couldn't help but admire his disposition. The mere mention of his name had invoked fear in the average gangster. Now that his reign of terror was over, his death was celebrated like the end of a cruel dictator. Unbeknownst to the Homies up North I anticipated the fury that would follow his departure; and the influx of criminal elements returning to claim a piece of the land. Unlike the average layperson criminals and gangstas represented independence with disorder. During the first month local news reported violent crimes had doubled; the second month it had quadruple. In a fierce campaign to curve the violence, Pastors and Politicians' assembled daily marches, while state, local, and federal law enforcement detained and arrested anyone they suspected of doing wrong. Just as quick as they shut down one Crack house, two more were being open. Just as quick as they taped off one murder scene, another unfortunate victim was closing his eyes for the last time.

Dad's was a neighborhood favorite; a breakfast, lunch, and dinner spot by day, and a bar and dance hall at night. Unbeknownst to anyone besides Lil Bull it was also my first legitimate acquisition; and the location of my first official meeting as the head of CCO's Street Operations. CCO was one hundred and thirty-eight soldiers strong on the streets of America. Twenty-two were operating in Los Angeles; twelve were stationed in the Bay area; fourteen were posted in San Diego, while the rest were scattered across the United States. Out of the fourteen in San Diego Raw Dog from West Coast 30's presented the greatest threat, and more than likely would be the one they selected to come at me if they discovered what I was up to. Raw Dog was a young and dedicated soldier with dreams similar to my own. I knew him well, and prior to this latest turn of events looked forward to working with him. Over a year and the half had passed since I last seen him, which in the crime game was tantamount to a life time. Unable to fully trust him, and airing on the side of caution, I marked him for death.

I asked Raw Dog to arrive an hour early so I could have a one on one with him. I couldn't help but smile when he arrived. Much to my surprise very little had changed with his appearance; he was still hood, still gangster, sporting a white T, blue Dickie's, and a pair of white Chuck's with blue shoe strings. On the surface Raw Dog was a small man with a big man complex. A stone cold killer, but far from being a fool, and like most gangsters that were fortunate to emerge from San Quentin head first instead of feet first he recognized and respected power. I made no attempts to intervene when Lil Buggs stop him at the door and attempted to path him down. When he refused Mike Loc and Black Cal quickly surrounded him. After removing a 45 from his waistline Mike Loc escorted him to my table.

"Sorry for the inconvenience Cuz, this is a gun free establishment; you know alcohol and firearms don't mix. You'll get it back when you leave. How have you been?"

"I'm chilling Cuz." He said, obviously still upset by the intrusion.

"Relax baby boy, my house is your house. Would you care for something drink?"

"Yeah I'll take a double shot of Hen on the rocks." After a few sips Raw Dog seemed to relax and open up. He had an interesting tale to tell, one that involved isolation, frustration, a lack of respect, and a serious disconnect between him and Zuberi. On all accounts Zuberi was less than a stellar leader, one that placed the needs of his homies before his comrades. Unlike the penitentiary there were no check and balance, Zuberi's word was law, if you liked it or not. The more I learned the more pleasure I received for ending his life.

For a brief moment I felt sympathy for all the shit Raw Dog had endured under Zuberi's command; but just as quick as it came, it left. Raw Dog was marked for death, and there was no reason to entertain otherwise. True enough there were many qualities I liked about him, but the fact of the matter was, he couldn't be trusted.

"Cuz I'm so happy you're home and back on your feet." He said after a moment of reflection. "We need a comrade out here that's going to play it the way it's supposed to be played. I don't mean to speak ill on the dead, but I was happy as a motha fucka when I heard Cuz got his issue. You don't know how many times I thought about killing him; and I'm not the only one that felt that way."

"From what I gathered Cuz wasn't the only one playing outside party lines, and that's one of the reasons I asked you to arrive early. Contrary to what you may believe the homies up North are well aware of everything going on out here. Zuberi lost his way, and that's why he lost his life. To be honest they wanted each and every one of you gone. You know how the game go Cuz, rules are made to be followed, and gangbanging and dope slinging go against everything we believe in. Instead of being a part of the solution, you became a part of the problem. Considering everything that's going on out here it's easy to see how one could lose his way. I'm not making excuses, because I don't believe in them. What I'm saying is I do understand; but as you know I don't make policy I just enforce them. Today is a new day, and you've been granted a new lease on life. What you do with it is entirely up to you, but one thing you must understand you won't survive another fuck-up."

"I hear you Cuz, and you don't have to tell me twice. I know I've been fucking up, and I'm not going to sit here and hit you with some lame ass excuses. I appreciate you going to bat for me; and to keep it one hundred with you I was concerned when I heard you were coming home. I knew shit was about to change, and I knew for those that wasn't playing right there would be hell to pay. Cuz you know me, and I've never been one to take the easy way out. Whatever I have to do to make things right all you got to do is say so."

"I'm glad you feel that way. Our first order of business is to clean house; and first on the list is Monk, Spike, and Wolf Dog. How you manage to handle this is entirely up to you. I trust you will handle this quick and quiet."

"Cuz it's good as done." Raw Dog said with a gleam in his eyes. There was nothing more satisfying to a murderer than the opportunity to kill. I sat back and quietly observed Raw Dog as he contemplated the task at hand. The signs were visible, and there was nothing more disturbing or compelling than being in the presence of the devil. Unbeknownst to the average layperson there was a distinct difference between a killer and a murderer. While a killer killed out of necessity, a murderer killed out of pleasure. Raw Dog was evil by all means, and like most murderers I had the displeasure of coming in contact with I realized the quicker I killed him the better off I'll be.

Despite so many individual accomplishments in the crime game; most notable, The Uzi Gang, The Get Down Crew, The East Side Rollin 40's Crip Gang wasn't recognized as a formidable threat to any of the major sets; which in itself would come as a blessing; because the worse mistake a gang could make would be to underestimate the strength of an adversary. Far too long Neighborhood Rollin 40's sat back and watched as other gang's stake their claim on the city. Although we were the smallest of the five major sets, what the hood lacked in numbers we made up in wit. The hood was comprised of a unique set of criminals that specialized in kidnap and armed robberies but the majority of our casualties resulted from gang banging. True enough the hood was founded on the principles of Crip, but in actuality the majority of us were gangsters, and our alliance was strictly to the dollar bill.

I realized in order to prosper we had to separate ourselves from past affiliations and create a new body of gangsters that more accurately represented what we were all about. It was our time to rise, and I could think of no one more qualified than I to lead the charge. I was schooled by the best, Crip legends from every set. 1990 would mark the beginning of a new era in the hood. I realized not everyone would share my vision or be receptive to change, and more than likely a time would come when we'll have to deal with the naysayers. The beginning was always the most vulnerable stage, and the point in which the strongest challenge would come.

My reputation alone was enough to bring the homies to the table, but I realized it would take a lot more to convince them to stay. There was nothing more persuasive than the prospect of getting paid. I understood the most important stage in forming a criminal network was the selection of its founding members. It was essential these men were beyond reproach. One bad seed is all it takes to turn a dream into a nightmare with devastating consequences. I was acutely aware of the penalties associated with organize crime. The RICO act carried a minimum mandatory sentence of twenty years to life.

One thing about the East Side Rollin 40's Crip Gang there was never a shortage of hitters and go-getters on the streets at one particular time. Lil Bull was the first homie I shared my vision with, and not surprising Cuz was the first one to jump on board. Later that evening we invited Tye Stick, an O/G, who recently returned home after serving 7 years at Folsom State Prison. Standing 6 foot 5, tall and lanky, Tye Stick didn't have an athletic bone in his body. Not known for his fight game,

Cuz was quick on the trigger, and known to blast at the first sign of provocation. Mike Loc was a youngster, but was respected like an O/G. A straight clown when he was chilling, but quiet and serious when it was time to put in work. Everything about him represented Crip. Like Tye Stick he was also tall, but unlike Tye Stick, Mike Loc was physical and real aggressive. Lil Ron was the most serious out the group, quiet and laidback, he was short on words, but big on action. Bayshea was the coolest of the cool, a straight player, strictly about his money. Cuz was the type of homie you could hit the club with and sweat some chicks one night, and pull a robbery with the next night. Weazel was the youngest, but had the features and strength of a grown man. Five feet five and stocky as a bull, Weazel was considered a knock-out artist. After careful thought and painstaking consideration Lil Bull and I invited them to a private gathering. Without divulging too much we shared our concerns and the need for reconstruction in the hood. All seemed to be in agreement, but that was only the first of many steps. Right now these men were simply prospects, if by chance they survived the orientation phase. One thing they all shared in commons, they were all certified gangstas, born and bred in the Hood with strong family ties. They all paid their dues in Blood and Sweat; and each man been in the game long enough to know it was Blood In and Blood Out. But most importantly, these men were not only my homies, they were regarded as close friends, and I had much love for each and every one of them. As I stood at the door and embraced each homie as they left I quietly wondered if push came to shove, for the sake of the organization could I kill one if need be. It was a hypothesis I could not answer.

My lawyer informed me I was wanted for questioning as a result of the incident in which I nearly loss my life. I didn't need him to tell me in the majority of cases involving gang members; the State of California didn't recognized self-defense as a legal defense involving murder. At worse I was facing 2nd Degree Murder, and at best I was looking at a Felon in Possession of Firearm on top of a Parole Violation. He suggested I turn myself in and he promised to have me back on the streets in less than 3 years. I laughed like that was the funniest shit I heard in my entire life. He had lost his fucking mind if he thought for a second I would willingly surrender, knock on the door of the county jail and tell them to let me in. I informed him his services were no longer needed.

  Big Dee was a heavy weight, not just in size but also in stature. Recognized as one of the biggest crack dealer in the city Big Dee had more houses than the average dope dealers had cars. Constantly on the move only those in his closest circle were privy to his whereabouts on any given day. Lil Bull was a part of that circle.

  We pulled into the alley behind Big Dee's beach front property and found Boo, his trusted right hand man snug against a pretty, red hair white girl that didn't look a day over sixteen. After spotting us he gave her a pat on her rear and sent her on her way.

  "Pretty Boy welcome back Cuz; Lil Bull told us you were back on your feet, what took you so long to come around?" He asked and joined our side.

  "I've been laying in the cut trying to put this master plan together."

  "I hope it works out for you. You know if you need something, anything, we got you."

  "Since you mentioned it I could use a couple of ounces of that Cali Good."

  "You damn sure came to the right place, come on let's go inside."

  One thing Big Dee didn't take chances with was his security; and he was adamant that everyone, with the exception of Boo and Lil Bull submit to a full body pat down before entering his home. I lifted my arms and allowed one of his body guards to pat me down. After removing my 45 from my hostler, he glanced at Big Dee and handed it back.

  "Pretty Boy I'm happy to see you back in the midst, the game need niggas like you to keep these bitch ass niggas in line. You know if shit gets too hard to handle all you got to do is call, we coming." Big Dee said and meant every word.

"Appreciate the offer, but if I ever run into something I can't handle I won't live long enough to call anyone." I shot back and meant every word.

"I feel you on that; so what are your plans, you know I could always use a man of your caliber on my team."

"You know I've never been a good team player. I like to do what I want, when I want. It's kind of hard to do that when you represent a crew. But you know I don't have to be on your team to roll with you. You call, I'm coming."

Big Dee was a man of many indulgences, none more satisfying than his love for fine wine, fast women, and top grade weed. Known to be extremely generous to his friends, a casual visit quickly turned into a small private party with the invites of a dozen strippers, an assortment of drinks, and a platter of weed and cocaine for those that indulged.

"Pretty Boy lite this up," Big Dee said and handed me a weed pipe with a big fat bud sitting in the bowl. I fired it up and took a long, slow hit. After filling my lungs with smoke I tried to pass it to him. "No that's on you Cuz." He chuckled and everyone joined in on the laughter. I didn't know what was so funny. It wasn't until I took the second hit and blew the smoke out I realized the joke was on me. I was so high I couldn't see straight.

"What the fucks in this?" I asked, joining in on the laughter.

"That's Chronic!" Big Dee shouted and gave Lil Bull a high five.

"Come on honey." A petite brunette with a beach body took my hand and led me to the bedroom. Once there she disappeared inside the bathroom and returned a few minutes later wearing a see-through night gown with nothing underneath. She directed me to a leather swivel chair and turned it at an angel facing the bed. It was evident by her knowledge of the room she been here before.

"Take off your clothes." She whispered with a penetrating glaze exploring every inch of my nakedness with her soft green eyes. "Please sit down and enjoy the show."

Enjoy I did; I was mesmerized, trapped in a drug induced ecstasy. I could feel the softness of her body, and hear the sound of her moans as I penetrated her without ever touching her. She was a professional, an exotic, erotic dancer. My monster was rock hard with an overwhelming desire to fuck her like she never had been fucked before. She made no gestures for me to join her, therefore I remained in my seat watching her fingers explore the inside of her wetness until her juices erupted, leaving her spent and satisfied with a smile that illuminated the room.

"That was good." She softly murmured.

"Yes it was." I repeated as my monster jerked two times and shot a load that landed on her leg, which she quickly scooped up and licked every drop from her fingertips.

"The show is over, but I'm not finished, come here and give me some of that big black dick." She whispered seductively and spread her legs a little wider.

Still rock hard she didn't have to tell me twice. I rose to my feet, crawled between her legs and allowed her to guide me inside her pretty pink pussy. I never imagined sex could be this fulfilling. In spite of her moans or the enormous pleasure she was providing I maintained my restraint and pushed deeper and deeper into her snatch until my nuts refilled and shot an another load over her stomach. Completely spent I rolled over on my back and took her inside my arms. Not a word was spoken as she laid her head on my chest and stared into my eyes. She was mines, and we both knew it.

Cross Artist
Chapter 2

Pressure was known to bust a pipe, and was also the substance that separated the weak from the strong. I could feel the heat coming from every direction, but I wasn't tripping; lock, stock, and barrel I was all in. I was built for this shit. I recognized from Day-1 the Crime Game was the most dangerous occupation on the planet; and success was measured by longevity and securing a substantial amount of financial gains. The odds of achieving either were as astronomical as winning the lottery. For most it was like a rollercoaster ride, 5 years of fame followed by an untimely death, or worse, a life-sentence in a State or Federal Penitentiary. Nevertheless I was determined to succeed where so many others had failed. I realized in pursuit of ill-gains the profits never exceeded the risk; the more you wanted, the more you had to sacrifice. I wanted it ALL; therefore I was willing to risk it all; death or imprisonment versus a lifetime of riches, fast cars, and a flock of the most beautiful bitches.

My plate was full, just as quick as one enemy disappeared two more were added to the list. I kept my eyes opened and my ears to the ground. No one outside of Lil Bull and Felicia knew where I laid my head.

The fact of the matter Doc was still out there lurking behind dark skies plotting our demise. Lil Bull had employed two private eyes, one in Mexico, and the other in Los Angeles to track down Doc, Belinda, their family and close friends. In the meantime it was business as usual.

It had been over six months since I last seen Akeelah or received orders to kill Lil Bull and his family. As much as I wished this was no longer an issue, I knew the mere thought was wishful thinking. The clock was ticking and I was powerless to stop it. CCO had too many resources, and there were far too many variables to cover. I was just one of many hitters they could delegate for the job, and my greatest concern was them sending someone from L.A to finish the job. Just as I, Lil Bull was also moving under the radar. His family was in a safe location, which was one less worry.

I reserved a private room, candle lit dinner at Baci Ristorante, an Italian restaurant in Mission Valley. Akeelah once mentioned her fondness for Italian cuisine, and in an effort to impress, and show her not much got pass me I invited her to San Diego's finest. I rose to my feet and pulled out her chair when I observed her approaching. I couldn't help but admire her elegance; Akeelah carried herself with a grace one simply couldn't ignore. It was easy to see how most men would be intimidated by her; she was the true essence of a woman. A smile played across my face when we made eye contact, and I realized I was caught admiring her in a most seductive way.

"Good afternoon Ms. Akeelah." I said and open my arm.

"Good afternoon Jabari." She said and gave me a warm and affectionate hug. "I notice you don't respond well to Jabari, would you like me to call you Pretty Boy?'

"To be honest I prefer Pretty Boy, it's a name I've been known by my entire life. Jabari represent a man in captivity I'm free now."

"Pretty Boy it shall be. Now that we have that out the way I must say you look exceptionally well considering everything you've encountered since the last time we spoke."

"I feel exceptionally well."

"If you don't mind talking about it, I like to know if you learned who came at you. No one is claiming responsibility and the streets are not talking?" She asked with a look of concern.

"I appreciate your concern, but I have everything under control. Back to you, how have you been?"

"I've been worried to death. I'm mad at you; six months without a call left a lot for the imagination. I didn't know if you were dead or alive."

"I'm sorry. These last few months have been anything but pleasant. My number one objective was getting back on my feet, and in the midst of this gangsta shit, I had to go under in order to get back on top. You can inform the homies I'm back in top form and ready to push this shit the way it's supposed to be pushed."

"Speaking of the comrades, I'm sad to inform you they all been moved to Pelican Bay, the Department of Corrections new Super Maximum prison. We have yet to develop a secure line of communication. Right now everyone is operating in the blind. We have the smartest minds on top of it; therefore it's just a matter of time before we work it out."

"I'm sorry to hear that." I lied; this was a blessing in disguise, which meant I was operating on my own accord, with no one to answer to. How are you holding up?"

"I've seen better days, but I must say things are a lot better with you back in the picture." She said and placed her hand on top of mines. This time I didn't move.

"I'm glad you feel that way." I said and flipped my hand inwards and interlocked her fingers. One of the reasons I wanted to see you, the last time we spoke you left a lot to be desired."

"I hope it was pleasant." She said and continued to smile.

"It most certainly was, and I must admit despite my greatest efforts I simply couldn't stop thinking about you. When I think of you I see everything I ever wanted in a companion. Not only are you extremely beautiful, sexy in a way that entices me; you're strong, but yet so subtle, intelligent with an equal amount of street savvy. On all account you're perfect for a man like me. But as fate would have it, you're already taken, at least to some extent. For the past few months I have thought long and hard how could I have you without violating everything I hold near and dear to my heart. I understand your situation, and I can live with that. What I can't live with is being your boy toy, somebody you turn to when the need arises. What's business is business, and what's personal is personal. In order for you and I to take a closer look at each other it must be understood what we share on a personal level must remain private; between you and I, and no one else. Is that possible?"

"Yes, that's more than possible, and to be honest I would prefer it that way." It was obvious by the look in her eyes she was venturing into an area that wasn't new, but still so exciting. In spite of her strengths, deep down inside she was a woman in need of affection; the type of affection that only a man of enormous strength and character could give her. I was fond of Akeelah; she was like a breath of fresh air, and a sheer pleasure to be around. As enjoyable as I found her to be, I held no doubts whatsoever if the situation demanded I would kill her quicker than a heartbeat. In the meantime I planned to explore every facet of her life; although the physical attraction was strong I was more interested in learning what was inside her head.

"Have you decided what you like?" I asked and folded the menu and placed it on the edge of the table.

"I'm famished; there is so much to choose from, what would you suggest?"

"My instincts tells me you're not big on red meat, therefore I would suggest the Pollo Marsala, the chicken is absolutely delicious." I smiled and licked my lips as if it was one of my favorites.

"That sounds like a wonderful suggestion." She returned my smile and stared into my eyes, growing more impressed by the second. I did my homework, and by being a man of detail every small gesture was designed for a particular response. For myself I selected the Filetto di Manzo al Pepe Nero, a Filet mignon, the perfect dish for a steak lover. By the time the meal arrived we were finishing up our first bottle of wine. Everything was going according to plan.

The stars were lined up and the horizon never looked more promising as it did at that moment. I had a plan, one that involved symmetrically eliminating all my enemies and taking over the city. It was a daring move, one that would require a skillful mindset; and a little luck. One of the first lessons Askari taught me was the Laws of Gravity; meaning every action will bring a reaction, followed by a counter action. At the age of twenty-five I considered myself a mastered Chess player, capable of comparing wits with the best of them. Unlike most criminals I was still a student of the Game, constantly searching for better ways of doing things. I studied crime and criminals like a criminologist; but unlike a criminologist I wasn't afforded a misdiagnosis. Calling the wrong play at the wrong time could very well have devastating consequences.

Staying ahead of Doc and law enforcement required me to be vigilant at all times. No one knew the moves I was making, or when I was making them. I was subject to pop up on you in a moment's notice, and whatever business I had with you, you better be ready, and more importantly you better be in good standing. It was all business and no pleasure, and that was one of the main reasons I decided to attend Big Dee's 40th birthday party that was being held at his lavish estate in Malibu.

Big Dee was an O/G from Long Beach Insane Crip Gang who met Lil Bull while serving a twenty year stint at Tracy, the Dual Vocational Institution. It was there they became cellmates and fast friends, which lead to a lucrative partnership once Lil Bull was released. I liked Big Dee and had much respect for him, but the fact of the matter his days of pushing that poison in my city was over. Although Lil Bull and I was closer than Siamese Twins I knew he would never approve a move on Big Dee; nevertheless there was nothing he could do stop it.

The party was in full bloom when we arrived. I stopped at the stage and was captivated by The Dramatics soothing the crowd with one classic after another. It was obvious by the way the crowd was slow grinding to the smooth melody I was not the only one that held the Dramatics in high esteem. We found Big Dee working three grills at the same time. I never met a big man that didn't love to cook just as much as they loved to eat. After seeing us approach he removed his apron and handed it to his daughter whom I met on a previous occasion.

"Happy birthday Big Cuz," I said and embraced the Big Homie.

"Thank you, glad you could make it. My home is your home. There is plenty of food, drinks, and women, but before you get loose I'd like to have a word with you."

I followed Big Dee inside his lavishly decorated home where he led me to his study. Big Dee was living the life that most gangstas only dreamed about. Lil Bull had mentioned he wanted to speak to me, but he didn't say why.

"Pretty Boy as I am quite sure you know San Diego is going through a transition. With the death of Zuberi and Lil Man southeast is wide open and in desperate need of a connection. It's my aim to fill that void. I know you're not about the Crack Game, and I will never suggest you join it. Lil Bull informed me that you have a unique set of skills behind the wheel and suggested you might be interested in a position I have available. The short version is I need someone to move some supplies from Long Beach to San Diego twice a month. If I haven't sparked your interests say so and we can terminate this conversation right now."

"By all means continue." I said and paid attention to every word. I couldn't have asked for a better situation. In the process of trying to accumulating the information I needed to come at Big Dee, I had to figure out a way to do it that didn't involve Lil Bull or me officially joining his squad; to that end he just solved a major dilemma brewing inside my mind. At the conclusion of our meeting he informed me he had a car packed and ready to be transported and would I mind making my first run tonight. I gladly accepted.

It was just turning dark when I pulled into the parking lot of Felicia's new home. Under my guidance Felicia made some major moves; not only did she secure a townhouse and a car, she learned how to stack her money, which had grown considerably. Every test I put her through she passed with flying colors. Six months to the day had passed since I last seen or played between Felicia's legs, and I couldn't deny the mere thought of dicking her down aroused me in a way that brought a smile to my face. It was time to sit her down and really see where her heart and mind was at. A true commitment, hood style or otherwise, always came with a conversation and a pledge.

I knocked on the door and covered the peep hole the moment I seen a shadow appeared. "Who is it?" Felicia asked.

"The man of the house," I answered. The door swung open and Felicia flew in my arms so fast she damned near knocked me down. "Come on baby let me take a look at you." I whispered in her ear hoping she released the death grip she had around my neck.

"I should be mad at you," she said and ran her hands down my face. "Why you didn't tell me you were coming home today?" She was ecstatic, happy beyond all measures, with a tenderness inside her eyes that was so powerful it left a warm feeling inside my chest.

"I wanted to surprise you." I said with a trace of truthfulness.

"Well you did, and it is a wonderful surprise. I miss you Pretty Boy." She whispered and surrendered to my touch. Damn I couldn't believe how wonderful her body felt pressed against mines. At twenty years old Felicia was by far the most demanding lover I ever had. Without another word being spoken she took my hand and led me to the bedroom. I stood still and allowed her to undress me and explore every inch of my body with her hands and lips. I wanted her just as bad as she wanted me. I backed her onto the bed where I removed her shorts and panties in one single motion. Without delay I crawled between her legs and allowed her to guide my massive hard on inside the entrance of her love nest. I pushed in slowly expecting to feel the tightness one would expect from a woman that hadn't had sex in six months. Instead I found a wound stretched far beyond my capabilities. A sickening laugh escaped my lips as I pulled out and rose to my feet.

"Baby what's wrong, why did you stop?" She asked while searching my eyes.

"You're a cold piece of work; and here I thought you might be the one."

"Baby what are you talking about?" She asked, her voice trembling with fear.

"Bitch don't play stupid; think about it, I'm sure you'll figure it out." I said and put my clothes back on.

"Where are you going?"

"To clear my head, and think about my next move."

In all my years of living I never held a woman to unreasonable expectations. Felicia was a beautiful young lady with an insatiable appetite for sex. Prior to the attempt on my life we were having sex six-seven times a day. I would have been naive to believe her strong desire for sex would simply fade because I was missing in action. What troubled me was the fact I was only gone six months; and in my eyes any bitch that couldn't keep her legs close for that short period of time was weak; and weakness was something I simply couldn't tolerate. I hated the fact her indiscretions diminished my perception of her. She lost a lot of points with this one, points I wasn't sure she'll ever be able to recoup.

Sleeping on the couch was not how I envisioned my first night back in her life. I needed some time alone, a little space to digest and analyze the situation. Regardless of my personal feelings Felicia was still an intricate part of my plans to build a squad of female killers. After careful consideration I realized I couldn't afford to push her away, nor could I allow her to go unpunished. I had to figure out a way to bend her without breaking her. I had to teach her a lesson and make her understand this wasn't baseball; her next strike would be her last strike.

Once my initial rage subsided and I had a clearer perspective how I would play her, I returned to the bedroom and climbed between the sheets, stopping just short of touching her. I was so close I knew she could feel my breath on the back of her neck. Unable to restrain herself Felicia backed her body into mines and took my arm and held it tightly around her mid-section. Her body slowly relaxed and she fell quietly asleep.

The awkwardness from the previous night had a lingering affect in the morning. I couldn't deny the situation bothered me immensely, which was obvious by my silence.

"Good morning Floyd." She said and sat my breakfast in front of me.

I gave her a quick nod and turned my attention towards the grits, eggs, and sausage.

"So this is how you're going to act?" She asked, refusing to leave well enough alone.

"Believe me baby this is not an act. But since you're in the mood to talk sit down and let's have a conversation."

"Why are you looking at me like that?" She asked still standing.

"Like what?"

"You look like you hate me."

"I don't hate you, I might not like you right now, but I don't hate you."

"I'm sorry baby, I swear I am."

"Sorry for what?"

"I'm sorry for hurting you."

"I'm not hurt, I'm disappointed. In one breath you confess your undying love and claiming to be my girl; than on the other hand you're out here giving your pussy a party like you're free and single. You can't have it both ways."

"I wasn't out here giving my pussy a party. I fucked one Nigga while you were gone; it was just a fuck and nothing else."

"I wouldn't give a fuck if you fucked a monkey; what I'm telling you is, you're not going to be out here representing my name and allowing a motha fucka to jump in and out your panties at the same time. That's some real disrespectful shit. You need to find out exactly what you want before we put a label on it."

"I know what I want; I want you, and I'll do whatever I got to do to prove it." No sooner than the words left her lips the doorbell rang.

"You can start off by getting the door." I said sarcastically. "I wonder who the fuck this could be?"

"I don't know; Pretty Boy I swear I never brought anyone over here."

After a brief glance through the peep hole Felicia stumbled away from the door with a look of sheer terror in her eyes. I could recognize fear at a moment glance. She was scared to death. I jump to my feet wondering what was going on. My first thought was the police. "Who is it?" I asked in a hush tone.

"Lori ex-boyfriend," She whispered. "That's the Nigga that tried to kill her."

I retrieved my 9mm and tiptoed to the door to see who it was. After glancing through the peep hole I placed my gun in the small of my back and opened the door. "Damn Cuz when you say early, you really mean early."

"Cuz this is the best time to handle business; hurry up and get dressed we got a lot of work to put in." Boo said and stepped inside the apartment.

"Give me about ten minutes." I returned to the bedroom and found Felicia hiding in the bathroom shaking like a wet puppy in fear of her life. Once she regained her composure I discovered prior to meeting Felicia and Lori, Lori set Boo up to get rob. When Boo refused to cooperate he was shot in the chest and left to die. It was a story I was all too familiar with. The only thing new was the identity of the woman who set him up. And by the way Felicia was reacting she was knee deep in the middle of this shit. I thought about taking her in the living room and confronting the issue, but decided against it. I wasn't privy to all the details surrounding the robbery. If Boo wanted Felicia's head there wasn't much I could do to stop him. In the hood it was considered a form of weakness to allow a bitch to come between two gangsters. It was best to leave things as they were, at least until I learned more about the incident.

Our first stop was a townhouse in Spring Valley. For the better part of the morning and the entire afternoon I watched Boo masterfully cut up 10 kilos of crack with the precision of a surgeon. It was evident by the manner in which Cuz went about his business he knew his work and he knew it well. Boo was what most would consider a professional crack dealer, and unlike most in the crack game he was fortunate he never seen a day in jail. He attributed his good fortunes to his knowledge of the game and a little luck. I agreed.

"You want me to cut theses up?" Boo asked referring to the two kilos Big Dee had promised me.

"Yeah cut them in quarters; eight nine ounce blocks."

Cooking and cutting crack wasn't a trade you could learn at school. It was a trade that was passed from one hustler to the next. Lil Bull showed me how to cook, and Boo showed me how to cut and package the product. Boo was slow but meticulous. Once everything was packaged and ready for transport we went about the mandatory task of cleaning up. Using a bleach base cleaning solution we wiped down every inch of the kitchen and swept and mopped twice. Satisfied everything was in order we exit the house with two gym bags both containing 180 ounces of crack, and another bag containing 1512 grams of heroin, plus my backpack with eight quarter kilos.

We came in a Ford Taurus and left in a Ford Mustang. Boo suggested I drive which I gladly accepted. Boo directed me to a house in Lemon Grove. Just as we were pulling up a moving truck with two black dudes were just leaving. I stared at the driver who looked awfully familiar but I couldn't place his face. I was certain I knew him, and I had a funny feeling it wasn't on friendly terms.

"You know them cats?" I asked Boo.

"Yeah they're cool, that's my girl's people."

I stayed in the car with my gun in my lap and the engine running while Boo unloaded the supplies. Although Lemon Groove was a predominately a white area it was still considered part of the Skyline Eastside Piru Gang. To add to my concerns a white station wagon pulled up and blocked me in. I hit my horn to signal the car to let me out. When it didn't move I emerged from my car, gun in hand and noticed it was a woman and two small kids occupying the car. I immediately concealed my weapon and asked the woman to let me out, in which she did. Boo had a reputation of putting a ready-made family inside a safe house; it was his belief a family would less likely draw suspicious. That may have been true in the eyes of society, but in the game it was a security risk. He had absolutely too many people privy to the location. He swore up and down no one knew his business and his girl didn't speak on household matters with her family or friends. As sharp as Cuz was there were some things he did that made no sense.

It was close to midnight when I arrived back at Felicia's, and as expected she was wide awake waiting on my arrival.

"Pretty Boy you been gone all day, I was worried to death, Daddy have you eaten?"

"I'm good; check it out baby I need you to handle some business." Without as much as a thought Baby Girl got up, eager and ready to do whatever Daddy asked her to. I gave Felicia the backpack and instructed her to put it in a locker at the Grey Hound station until we found a safe spot to hide it. While Felicia went to handle business I shot to the hood. My last two brushes with freedom I tried to stay away from the hood believing I had a better chance at lasting in an area I wasn't known in. I was wrong. The most safest and secure spot for any gangsta is the area he knows best, his own neighborhood.

While most people were getting ready for bed, most gangstas were just getting out and about. I pulled up at Big Anthony's house and could hear the sound of loud laughter coming from the garage which was converted into a game room. I crept down the side of the house and noticed the door leading to the garage was slightly ajar. The homies were slipping in a serious way. Had I been an enemy I could have barged in and laid everyone down. Moving on the side of caution I knocked four times before I entered. It was never wise to surprise a room full of gangster, some of whom respond quickly at the slightest sign of aggression.

"Check you out, sitting here high as a motha fucka and straight slipping." I said as I stepped inside the room and greeted each homie with a hand shake and a hug. In attendance were Tye Stick, Lil Buggs, Lil Ron, Kenwood, and Black Cal. As we sat there smoking weed and sipping on Hennessy I couldn't deny how much I missed hanging out with the homies, talking shit, and reminiscing on past misdeeds, there was never a dull moment. It wasn't until the conversation shifted to making money that I was reminded exactly who I was in the company of. These men weren't drug dealers; they were robbers, which was a trait we all shared in common.

"Pretty Boy what's up with you, and this big money plan you was talking about?" Tye Stick asked, placing all the attention on me.

"I'm working on something right now." I said and gave them a play by play of the events that transpired in the last 24-hours. Suddenly the room fell quiet and the laughing and joking were replaced by a more serious discussion.

"Cuz we could hit that Nigga tonight!" Tye Stick said excitedly.

"Cuz I haven't had time to peep the situation or formulate a plan." I shot back and downed the last of my Hennessy.

"Cuz what is there to peep? All we need is an address, we got that. We have been riding down on Niggas our entire life; that's what we do."

As I searched my mind for the right phrase, a complete remedy of words to squash these irrational thoughts I could find none. The cat was out the bag and there was no putting it back. I paused for a moment and studied the faces around me, and couldn't believe even I was becoming increasingly drawn into this ill-advised plan.

There was a consensus almost immediately. The plan to rob Boo quickly took on a life of its own. While Tye Stick and I formulated a plan, the other homies went about gathering the tools we'll need to execute the move. We decided our best approach would be a full scale assault. Hit the house in the same manner the police would if they were raiding it. Kick in the door hollering Police! Police! Police! By the time they realized we weren't the police it would be too late. For obvious reasons I was the getaway driver.

Three hours later we were six deep in a stolen Suburban heading East; it was nearly 2am when we arrived at Boo's house. Based on the formation and size of the window frames leading from the living room to the back of the house I surmised there were three bedrooms with the master bedroom the last room on the right side of the house. The most dangerous part of a home invasion was the initial entry. It was imperative everyone in the house be accounted for. The fact that we were working with incomplete data increased the probability of someone getting hurt or killed.

Armed with an AK-47, two M-16's, and several hand guns the homies converged on the target. From the interior of the Suburban I watched as Lil Ron kicked the door off the hedges. Without delay the homies storm the house one behind the other. The fact I heard no gun shots meant they received no resistance. As I waited for the homies to return I had a quiet moment to reflect on my wild and reckless behavior. I couldn't believe I played my hand the way I did. I made a rash decision; one that I was sure would have lasting consequences. Had I thought about it a second longer, there is no way I would have participated in such an ill-advised scheme.

I snapped back to reality when I observed the homies exit the house. It wasn't until I observed Lil Buggs carrying a gym bag I knew the robbery went off as planned. The robbery was over but the getaway wasn't. Everyone still needed to be on full alert until we reached our destination.

It wasn't until we arrived back at Big Anthony's house, I learned Boo wasn't home and the homies only got one gym bag containing 180 ounces. After hearing a play by play account on what transpired I immediately recognized the ploy. Boo's girl played them like rookies. She gave them just enough to pacify them. I was mad as a motha fucka. I specifically told the homies what was inside the house, why they failed to grab everything was beyond my understanding. One hundred and eighty ounces of crack was a nice lick for the homies, but it wasn't worth the risk or the backlash I knew would follow. Anyone that was privy to the location would be a suspect. From there it would be a process of elimination. The fact that I was the new man in the crew would place me high on the list of suspects. The heat came immediately, by the time I arrived back at Felicia's my pager was going off like a Las Vegas slot machine. Four-seven, nine-eleven, nine-eleven, nine-eleven, four consecutive times, meant an extreme emergency. Four-seven was Lil Bull personal code, and nine-eleven three times meant I need to talk to you ASAP.

I pulled inside the garage and was immediately confronted by Felicia. "Hurry up!" She yelled from the doorway. "Kenny is on the phone." She said. "He said it's real important." I handed Felicia 180 ounces of crack, and paused for a moment before I picked up the phone. No one knew me better than Lil Bull, if I could convince him I didn't have anything to do with the robbery, convincing Big Dee would be a cake walk.

"What's up baby boy?" I said as casual as possible.

"Cuz we got a problem." He said in a hush tone.

"What the deal Cuz?"

"Boo got hit." He said and left it at that.

"Hit, what do you mean hit, is he dead?"

"Nah he got robbed."

"Cuz you got to be bullshitting. I just left Cuz a few hours ago everything seemed cool."

"I don't know what happened, but Big Dee wants everyone at the spot."

"I'm on my way."

"Pretty Boy," he whispered and paused.

"What's up Cuz?" I asked, concentrating on every word.

"There's no easy way to ask you this. Me to you Cuz, did you have anything to do with this?"

"Hell no Cuz, is that what Boo is saying?"

"No Cuz he's not saying that, the thing is, Boo just moved into the spot yesterday and only a handful of people knew where it was, you just happened to be one."

"Check it out Cuz I'll be there in twenty minutes."

"I'll see you when you get here, and Cuz, be prepare for anything." There was nothing else left to say, Lil Bull final words summed it up. I hung up the phone and found Felicia standing behind me. I opened my arms and she slid her soft body inside my embrace.

"Baby please don't go, I got a funny feeling about this." She pleaded and wrapped her arms tightly around me. I wished it was that simple.

"I got to go, there's no way around it." I said and kissed her on her forehead.

"Well I'm going with you." She said defiantly like her presence would make a difference.

A light laughter escaped my lips and a smile appeared on my face. "Baby I need you to go put this up, and if by chance this shit get ugly, and I don't make it back, sit on this shit a whole year, than get your money."

"Baby what's going on, please don't talk like that." She pleaded and started crying.

"I was just playing." I whispered, knowing in my heart that was the realist shit I said all day.

Lil Bull and Big Dee were standing outside when I pulled up. More than likely Big Dee followed Lil Bull outside to get a firsthand look at my reaction upon learning what had taken place. I removed the safety on my 9mm before I stepped out the car.

"What's up Cuz?" I said as I approached them making sure I made eye contact with Big Dee.

"It been a long day and I got a feeling it's going to be an even longer night." Big Dee said and shot me a glance. "Lil Bull told you what went down?" He asked, scrutinizing my every move.

"All he said was Boo got jacked and I needed to get here ASAP."

"Yeah, some Niggas kicked in the door and jacked Boo for ten kilos of coke and a key and a half of heroin." Big Dee threw it out there to see how I would respond.

"Damn Cuz that's a lot of shit. There's no way in the world a Nigga would have taken shit from me, I don't give a fuck how many Niggas it was. Cuz you mean to tell me Niggas got away with all that dope and no one is dead. Cuz you got to be kidding me?" I said pretending to be upset Cuz surrendered the goods without a fight.

Ten kilos of crack and a kilo and the half of heroin, Boo turned out to be a slick motha fucka. I wasn't mad at him I would have did the same. Cuz cuffed more than we took. Cuz stole from the hand that feeds him; if he didn't she did.

"Pretty Boy when you dropped Boo off did you see anything out of the ordinary." Big Dee asked, still scrutinizing my every move.

"To be honest Cuz the only thing I was looking for was anything with red on. You know them Skyline Niggas be deep around here." I kept it short; knowing a guilty man would try to place suspicion on someone else.

"Come on lets go inside." Big Dee suggested.

Throughout all my years in the crime game there was nothing in my past that would have prepared me for the atrocities I was about to witness. Sitting in the middle of the room, completely nude and strapped to a chair was the battered and bruise body of Boo's girlfriend. At first glance I thought she was dead until I heard her muttered something I couldn't understand.

"Cuz she doesn't know anything." Boo pleaded.

"Nigga if I was you I'd worry about my own ass." Big Dee said with a hint of savagery that left no doubt everyone was fair game. "Cuz before we leave this motha fucka you can bet your ass I'm ma know exactly what happened to my shit. Dog wake that bitch up!"

"Dog removed a vial from his pocket and placed it under the woman's nose reviving her instantly. "Bitch I'm tired of playing with you. Bone, go grab one of her kids." Big Dee ordered.

"Please God no! Please don't hurt my babies!" The woman pleaded.

"Bitch shut the fuck up." Dog said and slapped her so hard it felt like the house shook.

I quietly wondered did Bone consciously select the little girl over the little boy who just happened to be the youngest. Even at the tender age of two it seemed like the little girl knew something was terribly wrong. Bone was Big Dee chief enforcer that mainly dealt with in house discrepancies. He wasn't a social individual, and rarely interacted with anyone in the crew. I guess there was no sense getting close to someone you might be later called on to kill.

Bone sat the little girl between her mother's legs and she immediately started crying. I glanced at Lil Bull who also appeared agitated by what was taking place. I wasn't concerned about the woman because she made a conscious decision when she chose to get involved with a drug dealer. But the little girl didn't have a choice in the matter. Deep in my heart I knew I couldn't stand by and watch harm come to this child. I also knew in order to stop it I would have to kill almost everyone in the room. The more I thought about it the more outrageous it appeared. Big Dee had seven gun slingers posted around the living room, not including himself, and Lil Bull.

"Bitch open your mother fucking eyes and pay real close attention because I don't want you to think this is a trick or something!" Big Dee yelled and held up two bullets and placed them inside the chamber of a 38 revolver. With a quick spin and slight flip of his wrist the chamber fell back in place. "This is how this game is played. Every time I ask you a question and you give me the wrong answer I'm ma put the gun to your daughter's head and pull the trigger. First question, where is my dope?" He asked.

Time seemed to travel with lighting speed as a sudden feeling of fright overwhelmed me. I locked eyes with Lil Bull searching for a sign that would support these irrational thoughts racing inside my head. I reached inside my waistline and Lil Bull bowed his head and shook it from side to side.

"Bitch you have ten seconds." Big Dee shouted and placed the gun to the little girl's head. "Ten, nine, eight-," the countdown begin. Hysterical beyond measures the woman began to rant and rave like a mental patient. It was clear she had lost all sense of reality. "Seven, six, five-," the countdown continued. "Four, three, two, -."

"Hold up Cuz!" Boo shouted. "The dope is in the basement."

Nigga I knew you had something to do with this from the gate. You were too nervous. Nigga me and you go all the way back to grade school and this is how you play me; you steal from me." Big Dee said with a calmness that left a chilling effect on the room.

There was no reason to stick around; it was a family matter now, one that only Big Dee and his inner circle could resolve; and besides I didn't want to be nowhere in the vicinity when Big Dee learned he was still 180 ounces short. I stepped outside and took a deep breath, the air tasted crisp and clean, it felt good to be alive.

It's not a Game
<u>Chapter 3</u>

In my 26 years of living I have known a great deal of despair, it comes with the territory. In my world bad shit happens to bad people all the time. The realization that Boo and his girl met their demise on account of something I initiated didn't bother me in the least. Pity was a sentiment no gangster could afford to exhibit. In Boo's situation he bet his life against a kilo and a half of heroin and five kilos of cocaine. To me that was a reasonable bet, I for one have waged my life against far less many times.

The following day Big Dee sent Lil Bull to retrieve his car. Unable to determine who clipped him for the other five kilos he severed his ties with anyone that was privy to the location. I wasn't tripping; nor was I finished with him. Any one that played the game the way Cuz did was bound to get fucked over in the end.

Summer 1988 East Side Rollin 40's Crip Gang was in full force on the streets of Southeast. While most gangs relied on the crack game to generate funds, in the hood we relied on kidnaps and armed robberies. In the hood it was easier to assemble a crew of robbers than it was to put together a two on two basketball game. I promised to keep the homies busy, and busy they were, robbing everyone we believed were involved in ill-gains.

The NO GOOD HOOD is what our enemies called us, and with good cause. I would be the first to admit most of the homies were on some serious bullshit and bear watching at all times. The homies weren't the type you invited to the house to catch a game, or the type you introduced to your family; they were the type you rob, kidnap, and kill with. What made the hood San Diego's most dangerous gang was the fact we had so many criminal elements operating independent of each other. As small as the hood was we were probably responsible for eighty percent of the robberies taking place in the city.

Just as some were marked for robbery, others were marked for murder. Raw Dog had handled his business exceptionally well, so well I was inclined to give him a pass. Had he not been the driver when CCO made an attempt on Lil Bull's life I may have been inclined to do so. Once again he appeared agitated by the patted down and removal of his firearm when he entered Dad's. Unlike before the bar was relatively empty for the exception of a few homies. A smile played across his face when we made eye contact.

"Have a seat Cuz; you care for something to drink?"

"You know it, a double shot of Hen on the rock." He said with the confidence of a man absence of any concerns.

"A double shot of Hen on the way. I must compliment you Cuz, I like your work, and I couldn't have put it down any better."

"You know me Cuz, I aimed to please."

"I'm happy to hear that because I got another job for you." I said and paused at the sight of Lil Buggs approaching with his drink. Caught up in the moment Raw Dog didn't notice Lil Bull approaching from behind. In one swift motion Lil Bull placed a half-nelson around his neck and extracted him from seat. All the struggling in the world couldn't save him as I quietly watch Lil Bull snap his neck like a rag-doll. By the time Lil Bull released him Raw Dog was no longer among the living.

Since the beginning of time the hood had always been divided between Four-Seven Block Gangstas and Forty-First Street Hustlers. There were light weight scrimmages from time to time but nothing serious. That was until a hustler on Forty-First Street told a gangsta from Four-Seven Block he couldn't hang on 41st Street. We took offense, and sent them a message by robbing Pee Roll their most vocal critic.

Pee Roll had proved to be the first in a string of robberies that ripped the hood apart. Once we started robbing our own homies it became apparent anyone with a dope sack was fair game. We didn't give a fuck if you were black, white, Cuban, Mexican, Crip or Blood if you were in the business of selling drugs you were fair game.

Robbing drug dealers was turning out to be a lucrative business. We were coming up on so much cocaine we were forced to jump in the Crack Game just to get rid of it. It was never my intentions to stop the flow of Crack, but to redirect it. You could sell anywhere you wanted to sell you just couldn't sell in my Hood.

I introduced Felicia to the hood, not as my girl but as my partner in crime. The homies weren't use to seeing a female villain, especially one as young and sexy as Felicia. After schooling Felicia on the fine arts of surviving, and arming her with a small caliber 32 I put her in charge of distribution and sat her and three of the homies in a dope spot on the outskirts of Downtown San Diego. Contrary to what the local news reported there were twenty times more white crackheads than blacks, which was evident by the amount of sales. Word quickly spread, in actuality turned into ideal situation for most whites that were uncomfortable travelling to a black neighborhood to score.

Regardless how much money we were making in the crack game we were still pulling off at least two robberies a week. It was only a matter of time before the streets started talking. Once you acquired a certain reputation in a certain field you were bound to get credit for a lot of shit you had no involvement with. Although it was good for the ego, it was bad for security because it made enemies out of people you never harmed.

A whole lot came with being a robber; the profession alone required you to be vigilant at all times, quick on your feet and even quicker on the trigger. Armed robberies to a robber were like crack to a crack head. It was an addiction that always started off good and always ended bad. I never met anyone who did one robbery and stopped. After a while it wasn't about the money; it was more about the act, the sadistic pleasure one received from having complete dominance over another individual, especially another gangster. There was no better feeling than making another tough motha fucka bow down on his knees and stripped of all his worldly possessions.

I was surprised to find Lori sitting in the living room when I arrived at Felicia. The last time I saw Lori was over a year ago; since then she had a child by one man but living with another. I always liked Lori because she never pretended to be anything other than what she was, a certified hoe.

I studied her carefully as she spoke candid about her boyfriend's business. The longer she talked the more obvious it became her boyfriend did nothing that remotely justified the hell she was trying to unleash on him. Based on what she was telling me, her boyfriend put her out because her funky ass refused to clean up.

"Lori I'm pretty sure you're telling me all this for a reason. Maybe if you cut through the chase and tell me exactly what you want I might be able to help you."

"I'm telling you all this because you're my boy and I know you like robbing Niggas, and I want you to rob him and kick his ass real good."

Lori's ex-boyfriend was an old school hustler name Moe who was twice her age and ran a legalized poker house on Market Street. Moe was a legend on the streets of Southeast, with a reputation that went all the way back to my childhood days. Most robbers were reluctant to rob old school hustlers, some out a sense of respect, some out a sense of fear.

According to Lori every Thursday night the buy in were five thousand dollars and not a penny less. Because Moe and the majority of his players had criminal records Moe was adamant No Guns were allowed in his establishment. After spending a great deal of time around older hustlers I discovered the majority of them were arrogant to a flaw, and honestly believed they had already survived the worst days of their lives and were now untouchable. It was this belief, more than anything that motivated me to take a closer look at Moe.

I approached every robbery the same. Select a crew according to the job. Study the mark's every move, and strike at the most opportune time. Running surveillance was a tedious task that require countless hours of sitting, watching, and searching for a weakness in his routine. Moe had so many holes in his security I was surprised he survived the game this long without getting rob. Normally I would have sent someone inside to gamble but Lori gave us enough information about the interior layout I could have found my way around the place with my eyes closed.

I selected Lil Buggs and Kenwood for the lick; Kenwood for his intimidating size and strength, and Lil Buggs for his agile and sharp intellect. We all shared the same ideology when it came to robberies. Security and safety, first and foremost, and in the event something went wrong our number one priority was the getaway even if we had to leave the money behind.

From the moment the shop opened we counted a total of eleven heads entering. It was eleven people we had to account for immediately. Being that this was my lick I ran point. Armed with a pistol handle saw off I stormed inside the shop with Lil Buggs right behind me and Kenwood behind him. Moe had two tables in full operation, one with six players and the other with five. As I did a quick head count I spotted two of our old school homies in attendance. By the expression on their faces it was obvious they knew it was us behind the dark ski masks.

"Everyone put your mother fucking hands on the table." I shouted and quickly zoomed in on Moe who appeared upset by this obvious intrusion. "Nigga what the fuck is you frowning about, you got something to say?" All it took was a slight roll of his eyes for me to unleash a quick brutal assault that left Moe bleeding profusely from a huge gash above his eye and his four of front teeth scattered on the floor. In the robbery game sometimes it took an unprovoked act of violence to gain everyone's attention. This was one of those occasions.

"Pay attention." I said and circled the tables. "I'm not in the business of repeating myself. When I point at you, stand up and take three steps away from the table and strip naked. Leave your shit where you stand and sit your ass back down. You two, stand the fuck up!" I said and pointed to the two men that were sitting next to Moe.

Two by two they did as they were instructed. Just as quick as they came out their clothes Kenwood retrieved them and placed everything inside a huge trash bag. I saved the homies Joe and Mentree for last. They been in the game long enough to know right now was not the time to play tough. I could feel the blood racing through my veins as I ordered them to their feet. For a brief second Joe hesitated, I took one step forward and leveled the shotgun at his chest. There was no need to speak my eyes said it all. Much to my relief Joe rose to his feet.

The robbery went as planned. It was a bitter-sweet victory. After a lengthy discussion we decided to return Joe and Mentree's valuables and give them an equal share of the profits. This concession seemed to satisfy Lil Buggs and Kenwood, but as usual I was somewhat skeptical. How do you compensate a man for stripping him asshole naked and taking all his shit at gun point. Putting myself in their shoes I realized the gangster in me would never forgive them. Looking at the worse possible case scenario I advised the homies to lay in the cut until we got a better angle on the situation.

By the time the sun came up news of our devious deeds were the talk of the hood. Although the story had differed; depending on who was telling it, the message was the same. Lil Buggs, Kenwood, and I robbed the big homies, and we were good as dead. My first reaction upon hearing this was one of distrust. Joe and Mentree were old school hustlers and played by the rules of the game. Real killers moved in silence, I doubted very seriously they would issue death threats at three well known gangsters with a reputation for putting in work. If I had a problem with you; you would be the first to feel it, but the last to hear it. As unlikely as the verbal threat appeared it didn't eliminate the possibility of a real threat being discussed behind closed doors.

A pre-empt strike against Joe and Mentree was not an option. Although they were the heart of Forty-First Street Hustlers their love and respect extended throughout the entire hood. To launch an attack against them we would have to be all the way in the right; and right now we were dead in the wrong. It's been my experience in times of internal conflict the best weapon a man could employ was complete silence. Lay in the cut, watch and listen, and never give your adversary anything to feed off.

After three successful robberies Lori earned a seat at the table. Although she didn't participate in any of the robberies the inside information she provided was instrumental in our success. I never been one to look a gift horse in the mouth but I often wondered what motivated Lori to cross those closest to her. It wasn't the money because she refused to accept any, nor was it any misguided romantic fantasy she may have had because I kept everything strictly business. Whatever it was I planned to take full advantage of it.

I glanced up from my plate as Lori walked up. She was twenty minutes late so I ordered without her.

"What are you eating?" She asked and took a seat across from me.

"Chicken Alfredo, would you like me to order you a plate?"

"No I'm really not hungry, may I have a little of yours?"

"Certainly, as a matter of fact you can have the rest." I said and pushed the plate to her. For a brief second Lori just stared at the food, I sensed her feelings were hurt.

"Is something wrong?" I asked sympathetically. Bruised feelings or not there was no way in the world I was going to share the same eating utensils as Lori.

"No I'm okay." She said and looked up.

"Here let me help you." I said and picked up the fork and started feeding her. Lori's eyes lit up and she started blushing as she looked around the restaurant to see if anyone was looking. For a woman that wasn't hungry she ate every last bit. Lori was a hard woman to read. As hard as I tried to figure her out I couldn't. The only time I ever seen her exhibit any form of raw emotions was when she talked about her baby daddy. It enraged her that he didn't claim her child.

At first I was somewhat hesitant robbing him. At best he was a low level drug dealer worth less than twenty thousand dollars. Financially there was no incentive to rob him. For reasons only she knew she wanted him robbed; and in a slick kind of way she reminded me I owed her.

"So how was the honeymoon?" I asked in reference to her overnight stay at her baby daddy's house. It had been over three months since Lori last saw him, and I needed fresh intelligence to formulate a plan. I sat back and quietly listened as Lori told me everything she knew about her baby daddy, the man she called Roger.

I studied her carefully and tried to visualize everything she was telling me. The more I learned the more I regretted committing myself. The fact that Roger lived in the middle of a huge apartment complex presented a number of problems. The most serious was gaining access to his apartment without alerting his neighbors.

Against our best efforts we couldn't pin Roger down. He didn't have a job, nor did he have a set routine. Sometimes he didn't leave the house for two-three days. The more difficult the situation appeared the more determined I became. After a week of toying with it, it dawned on me I was approaching this from the wrong angle. Instead of searching for a location to abduct him, our best chance of gaining access to his apartment was knocking on the door. According to Lori, Roger was a certified trick and a sucker for a thin waist and pretty face.

At thirty years old Jena was considered an old hoe by street standards; but to the average john she was still relatively attractive and worth pursuing. Unable to compete with the much younger strippers Jena eventually retired and started boosting name brand clothes and selling them at half price. I couldn't think of no one better suited than her to slide under Roger. Not only was she a perfect fit she was also Kenwood's bitch.

One thing I always admired about Kenwood, Cuz was a man of his word and he was always on time. I often called upon Cuz when I needed a strongman to subdued or choke out a Vic.

"What's up Crip?" He asked and took a seat.

"Same shit different day. What are you drinking?"

"I'll take a double shot of Remy, straight up."

"What's the latest?" I asked and waved down the cocktail waitress.

"The word on the streets Joe got a ten thousand dollar contract on our heads. Everybody think we skipped town. I heard Joe been spending a lot of time at Dad's. If you want I can check it out."

"That won't be necessary; we got plenty of time to deal with Joe. I got something else in the midst. Lori put me up on another lick, there's not a lot of money involved, maybe twenty thousand tops and some weed and pills. I'm doing it more out of a favor to her than anything else. Lori tells me dude is a straight up trick; how would you feel sending Jena at him?"

"I'm cool with that. Right now she's broke as a joke and don't have the slightest clue how she's going to pay her rent."

"I thought baby girl was winning. The last thing I heard she was robbing the city blind. What happened?"

"She caught a case and copped out to a five years suspended sentence. The judge told her if she caught another case her ass is gone. She's scared to death."

"So what's going on with her, how has she been eating?"

"I been looking out for her, but that shit is about to play out."

"So how do you want to play it?"

"I think it'll be better if you approached her." He said. "I'm really not trying to fuck with her right now."

"I hear you big homie."

The following morning I was up bright and early. I tried calling Jena but her phone was disconnected. Jena lived in the territory of the 5/9 Brims, better known as the South Bronx, the oldest Blood gang in San Diego. I did a quick visual scan of the street and flipped the safety off my gun before I emerged from the car. With the exception of a few stray dogs the streets were deserted.

"If you're looking for Kenwood he's not here." Jena shouted through a dark window.

"Why I got to be looking for Kenwood, why I can't be looking for you?"

"Cause you ain't never come over here looking for me."

"I guess it's a first for everything. Are you going to invite me in, or should I come back later?"

"Give me a second, let me throw something on." She said and returned a few seconds later. "Come in Pretty Boy; you got to excuse the mess I'm in the process of moving."

"Where are you heading?" I asked.

"Atlanta, I got people on my daddy side down there. I got to get away from San Diego, I feel like I'm suffocating here."

"I can feel you on that. The reason I'm here I got a business proposition for you. I got a mark I need you to slide under." I said casually.

"Do I have to fuck him?"

"More than likely; what I need is for you to gain his trust, not to the extent he divulges family secrets, but to the point where he invites you inside his life. How you manage to achieve that is entirely up to you."

"That sounds too easy, what are you not telling me?"

"It sounds easy because it is easy."

"How much is the job paying?"

"It all depends how much we take him for. It could be anywhere from five thousand to ten."

"I can really use some travelling cash."

"That sounds like a yes."

"It is, when do I meet him?"

"Today, if you're up for it."

"I am. What's the plan?"

Hood Shit
Chapter 4

It had been over a month since we robbed Joe and Mentree; and it seemed like the more time elapsed the more comfortable Joe became. Believing he ran us out of town Joe became more vocal about the incident and seemed to relish at the thought that it was he that single handily subdued the biggest threat the hood had ever known and returned it back to a sense of normalcy.

Although under new management, and for the exception of a few new bartenders and cocktail waitress I handpicked very little had changed, and that was the way I wanted it. Dad's was one of the oldest and highly respected establishments in the hood. It was a neighborhood favorite where the homies congregated for drinks and conversation. A laid back environment and considered a neutral zone where attitudes and personal beefs were checked at the door.

We were right around the corner when I received word Joe had just arrived. Although we were heavily armed we had no intentions of harming Joe unless he made us. With the alarm to the back door deactivated Lil Buggs unscrewed the lightbulb covering the rear exit to prevent any light going inside the club when we opened the door. One at a time we slide inside the club without anyone noticing. Joe was sitting at the bar facing the main entrance when I came up behind him and sat in the stool next to him.

"What's up Cuz?" I said in a non-threatening tone. Joe turned immediately upon hearing my voice.

"Pretty Boy," he murmured like he'd just seen a ghost. Slowly he turned around and scanned the dark, scarcely crowded club and spotted Lil Buggs and Kenwood laying in the cut right behind him. Suddenly a discouraging look appeared on his face as he acknowledged we could have killed him if we wanted to.

"Relax Cuz; we're not here to harm you. What are you drinking?"

"Rum and coke," he said in a hush tone like the words got stuck in his throat.

"So what's the deal Cuz?" I asked.

"I don't know you tell me?"

"From where I'm sitting you're the one with all the answers."

"Nah I'm the one with all the questions."

"Ask me what you like."

"I want to know why you robbed a spot you knew we were in?"

"We didn't know you were in there. We were counting heads, not faces."

"You expect me to believe that?"

"I don't give a fuck what you believe. You asked me a question and I gave you an answer. Listen Cuz don't get this shit twisted, the only

13.

reason I'm talking to you is because I don't want to kill you. I came here to see what it'll take to make things right?"

"You can start by returning our shit."

"You got that, what else?"

"I believe ten thousand dollars would be fair compensation."

"That sounds reasonable. So we're straight?"

"Yeah we're straight." He said and extended his hand, which was a clear indication he didn't want any problems. The objective of this exercise was not about reimbursement, it was to simply show Cuz how easy it was to kill him if we so chose. The moment Cuz issued a threat against us he relinquished all property rights.

Dressed in the skimpiest business outfit one could imagine Jena knocked on Roger's door with a supply of Avon products. Not only did he invite her in, he did everything in his power to prolong her stay, even going as far as buying over three hundred dollars' worth of products. Using the skills she learned as a stripper Jena had Roger eating out her hands from the moment he answered the door.

"Is that him again?" I asked when her pager went off for the second time in five minutes.

"Yes that's him. I told you he's sprung, and I haven't given him any of this pussy yet."

"You mean to tell me dude is tripping like that and he ain't fucked?"

"That's exactly what I'm telling you. You'll be surprise the extreme some men will go to get inside a woman's panties."

"No I wouldn't. I know most of these cats out here are tricks. But check it out I heard today is Roger's birthday?"

"Yes it is how did you know?"

"Never mind that, do you plan on seeing him today?"

"Yes later tonight, he thinks I'm ma give him some."

"You know that might not be such a bad idea. As a matter of fact it'll be the perfect distraction." I said as I played the scenario out inside my head.

"Come on Pretty Boy, not on his birthday."

"Come on Pretty Boy, not on his birthday. Wow! You sound like you caught feelings for this trick. You mean to tell me I sent you to get him and he got you?"

"No it's not like that?"

"Check it out Jena you don't have to bullshit me. From the moment you sat down you appeared awfully cheerful. If Cuz is the reason behind your glow I'm not tripping, but please don't sit there and lie to my face."

"Yeah you're right, I like Roger, and I been struggling with a way to tell you. The last thing I want to do is disappoint you. I don't know what he did, or why you want to rob him, but honestly he doesn't have a lot of money. He sells a little weed and pills from time to time. I swear that's it; and besides he's so good to me and my kids. I think he might be my ticket out the game."

"Sounds like you have given this a lot of thought. I'm glad you did the math, and I'm quite sure you know how this shit is going to play out. Baby if you think for a second I'm ma let you play me like this you must have lost your rabbit ass mind."

"Pretty Boy I'm not trying to play you."

"Bitch shut the fuck up. I don't believe you have the audacity to come at me with this weak ass shit." I said as my mind raced against the clock. Given enough time I was sure Jena would realize even if she crossed me the odds of me retaliating would be slim to none. Why retaliate it would serve no purpose; if anything it would only create unnecessary problems.

I faulted no one but myself for sleeping on the job and allowing things to materialize in the manner in which it did. I understood what attracted Jena to the likes of Roger. Like most women Jena just wanted a man that cared and appreciated her. Roger was nothing like the hardcore gangsters she was use to dating. In the hood the homies didn't open car doors or pulled out chairs. Anything society deemed as gentlemen like, the homies seen as some sucker shit. After years of catching the short end of stick when it came to men, Jena was ripe and ready for a man like Roger. I wasn't mad at her for wanting a better life; she just couldn't get it at my expense.

Pressed for time I quickly devise a plan that consisted of Jena seducing Roger and leaving the front door unlocked. She assured me she would handle her end, and I promised her we would handle business in a way Roger would never suspect her. As Jena rose to her feet she reached inside her purse and removed a set of keys that had a big gold R emblem attached to them. Realizing what she just did, she stuffed the keys back inside her purse, but it was too late. She forced a smile and I nodded. Things were more serious than I had anticipated. Roger had only known Jena two weeks and she was driving his car and had full access to his apartment.

All the signs said stop and kill game. This was a clear example where the risk far exceeded the rewards. As hard as I tried to justify my involvement I couldn't. This wasn't about Lori or the fact I owed her this was about my word; and in the crime game a man's word was his bond; and the scale in which his character was measured.

With the exception of a strong wind whistling in the air all was quiet. Kenwood and I scaled the wall at the far end of the apartment complex and took different routes that lead to Roger's apartment.

"You ready?" I asked Kenwood as I rolled down my ski mask and retrieved my gun from its holster.

"I'm ready as I'll ever be." Kenwood replied and rolled down his ski mask.

I reached for the doorknob and felt a sudden surge of adrenaline race through my body. It was a powerful sensation that could only be compared to the height of a sexual experience. I pushed the door wide opened and carefully scanned the living room. Satisfied Jena didn't cross us we stepped inside the apartment and closed the door behind us.

Just as I instructed Jena left the bedroom door slightly ajar. I peeped inside the room and found Roger sound asleep while Jena was frozen with her eyes wide open. The moment she dreaded was finally upon her and there wasn't a damn thing she could do to stop it. I approached the head of the bed while Kenwood took up position at the foot just in case we had to subdue him. I reached over and tapped him several times on the bridge of his nose with my gun. He opened his eyes immediately.

"Nigga if you make one sound I'm going to kill you and your bitch. Do you understand?"

Roger stared at the barrel of the gun with a mixture of fear and disbelief. He was a nerdy looking dude, the type of cat that could sell drugs his entire life and never get caught. It was funny how most good guys were attractive to the bad girl type; and most good girls were attracted to the bad boy type. It was a fatal attraction that for the most came with regrettable consequences.

"Get the fuck up." I instructed, and snatched the covers from the bed. "Where are the drugs and the money?"

"Man I don't have…." My first blow caught him in the back of his head. The impact from the butt of my Colt 45 knocked him to his knees. My second blow laid him out. "Nigga get the fuck up!" I shouted. When he didn't respond Kenwood rolled him over, and we all stared in disbelief at what appeared to be the first sign of death. Lying on his back with his eyes wide opened Roger stared at the ceiling as blood continued to pour from the back of his head.

"Pretty Boy he have a plate in his head, I think you killed him." Jena uttered with her voice cracking with fear.

"Bitch you picked a fine time to tell me." I said and knelt down to check his pulse. "Fuck," I murmured. Just that fast a robber turned into a murder.

"I got to get the hell out of here." Jena shouted and rushed to put her clothes on. I shot Kenwood a glance, not a word was spoken as he slid behind Jena and choked the life out of her. To be on the safe side I snatched two pillows from the bed and threw one to Kenwood. Four bullets to the head satisfied any doubts we had concerning their existence. After a quick clean-up we made a quiet exit and disappeared into the night.

Felicia was sound asleep when I arrived at her spot; I stood at the side of her bed and studied her briefly. A smile played across my face as I quietly thought about the wonderful times we shared together. For a brief moment I thought about killing game, rolling the dice and see where they land. Airing on the side of caution, I decided against it; far too much was at stake, and if I was wrong there was a strong possibility I might not recover. I glanced at the clock; it was close to 3 am, and if I was going to make a move I had to make it now before the sun came up. I reached over and shook her lightly, she opened her eyes immediately.

"What's wrong Daddy?" She asked and stared at me through the darkness.

"It's all good love, but I need you to get up and ride with me." Without further thoughts or questions Felicia did as she was instructed. Five minutes later we were on the highway headed towards Lori, who also didn't question why I needed her on such short notice. I was happy to find Lori standing outside when we pulled up. She jumped in the back seat and I turned up the stereo to eliminate any conversation. In a moment of haste neither Felicia nor Lori noticed Kenwood trailing at a safe distance behind us?

Felicia immediately sat upright when I made a sudden exit down a dirt road on the outskirts of Camp Pendleton. I glanced in the rearview mirror and noticed Lori was still oblivious to the events materializing around her. It wasn't until I came to a complete stop and Kenwood snatched opened the back door panic sat in.

"Bitch gets the fuck out the car!" He ordered.

"Pretty Boy what….." Before she could finish her sentence she was airborne. I could see the fear in Felicia's eyes as she listened to Lori shout and scream for dear life. Suddenly a dead silence fell over the darkness and it became so quiet you could hear yourself breathing.

"Do you love me?" I asked and stared into Felicia's eyes, witnessing a mixture of fear and confusion.

"Yes I love you." She whispered, unable to control the flood of tears falling from her eyes.

"Do you remember last year when I asked would you kill for me?" I said, studying her every move.

"Yes, I remember." She answered, still unable to figure out where I was going with this.

"Well baby that time has arrived; Lori must go, and it's on you to take care of her."

"Daddy, Lori is my best friend, anybody but her." She pleaded.

"There is no one but her. With you or without you, Lori is good as dead. So how do you want to play it?" I asked and wondered did she realize any farther hesitation would in a sense mark her own death.

"Okay Daddy I'll do it." She looked up and came to terms.

Kenwood was standing at the trunk of the stolen sedan when we emerged from the car. I handed Felicia a 9mm and stood slightly behind her, close enough to disarm her if she tried some funny shit. I nodded for Kenwood to open the truck; and no sooner than the lid came up Felicia fired away. I studied her closely and was happy to observe she didn't close her eyes when she pulled the trigger; which was a clear sign she was ripe and ready to mold.

"My baby, my baby;" I whispered in her ear and removed the gun from her hand. On our way home I glanced at her several times looking for signs of distress, finding none I felt overwhelmed, like a proud father witnessing his child walk for the very first time. Instead of taking her

19.

home I took her to my place where we made love like it was our very first time.

Salt Rock
Chapter 5

Christmas was less than a week away and I felt no sense of excitement. To me Christmas was just another day. From the age of thirteen to twenty-six I missed so many they no longer held any meaning. It was a disheartening feeling, one that seemed to remind me of my many failures. Sometimes all it took was a special event to make a criminal take a look at his life and realize how discontent he really was.

In the crime game it was never about being happy; happiness was an illusion that eluded most gangsters. At best it was about being content; satisfied you were still breathing and free from the restraints associated with incarceration. I, like most gangsters embrace adversity; it was the fuel that lit my fire, but it was also the fuel that if I wasn't careful would eventually consume me.

Up to this point in my life I had been fortunate; fortunate I wasn't dead or worse condemned to a lifetime in prison. Only God knows how reckless and unrelenting I had been in pursuit of ill-gains. How I managed to survive the 1980's was a mystery to me. As disappointing as the 1980's were I was optimistic about the 1990's. The 1990's would represent the beginning of a new era. The era of the East Side Rollin 40's Crip Gang.

With each murder and robbery law enforcement seem to beef up the pressure by stopping, questioning anyone they thought had knowledge of my whereabouts. I had two lawyers on retainer, one ex-prosecutor now a high profile lawyer, and an ex-homicide detective turned lawyer with a booming private investigator firm. In spite of the many felonies I committed or was a suspect in, law enforcement didn't have shit on me. I was wanted for questioning, and a parole violation for not reporting. Even so the day to day constraints that came with being a fugitive was enough to make the average criminal turn himself in. This was the ugly side of the crime game, the side where your mind started playing tricks on you and it became extremely difficult separating a real threat versus the ones that was a product of your imagination. This was the side where the mail man looked like the police, and you trust no one but your closest homies. In order to survive you had to maintain a constant state of paranoia. You had to keep moving and never stop; sleep lite and react to the slightest sound. This was the flip side of the game; this was the life of a fugitive.

For the most part I welcomed the heat; pressure was known to bust a pipe, it was also the substance that kept a man sharp and on top of his game. Although law enforcement presented a problem, they were the least of my concerns; it was the wicked streets of Southeast that presented the greatest threat; the killers and guerillas laying in the cut hoping to boost their reputation by closing my eyes for the final time.

Even in exile I managed to return the Hood back to prominence. Everyone in my crew were living large, pushing new whips and enjoying more money than they ever imagined. The sales of crack or illicit drugs were non-existence on 4/7 Block. Just as quick as one of the homies tried to open shop we shut it down. Even so there were some that didn't believe fat meat was greasy, and continued to violate the Drug Free Zone; Salt Rock being the latest. Upon his return, after Zuberi ran him out of town, Cuz felt it was safe to come back and pick up where he left off. It had been over six years since I last saw the big homie, and my love and respect for him had not diminished. He had left word at several locations he wanted to holla at me; with things being the way they were, the situation didn't demand me to stop what I was doing to meet up with Cuz or anyone else that wasn't a part of my immediate crew.

Instead of sending one of my Shut-Down Crews to close the spot, Lil Bull and I decided to pay Cuz a visit. No sooner than we hit 49th street it was obvious by the crowd congregating in the middle of the streets Cuz was up and operating. Upon seeing us the majority of crack heads ran for cover, while others were so anxious to cop they didn't recognize the threat that was upon them. After forcing our way to the front of the line with two 9mm we were confronted by an off-brand neither of us recognized. We quickly disarmed him and forced him back inside the apartment where we found Salt Rock and another individual we didn't know hovering over a plate of crack. Lil Bull quickly drew down on the other individual while I held the other at bay.

"What's popping Cuz?" I turned towards Salt Rock, not certain of his response.

"Pretty Boy, Lil Bull!" He shouted and jumped up with a smile on his face like this was a reunion of old souls. I released his crony and met him halfway with a smile and a hug while Lil Bull remained vigilant.

"Cuz I been all over the Hood looking for you Niggas." He said and took a few steps backwards and took a long look, checking me out from head to toe. "Damn it's good to see you Cuz."

"Likewise Cuz," I said.

"What's up Lil Bull?" He shouted and rushed to greet him. Reluctantly Lil Bull released his hostage and returned Salt Rock's embraced. There was a moment of awkwardness, whatever beef Lil Bull had with Salt Rock was still visible years later. Everyone froze at the sound of a loud banging on the door. Salt Rock motioned for one of his side-kicks to get it. He returned a few seconds later and informed Salt Rock crack sales were lined up.

"You got to shut it down Cuz; this is a drug free zone." I interrupted, ready to enforce this new legislation by any means necessary.

"Cuz I heard about your work all the way in Seattle, I like what you're doing around here. Let me down the rest of this, and I will shut it down." He said, waving to a plate with about 4 ounces of crack cut up in small quantities.

"Afraid I can't do that. Like you said you heard about this all the way up in Seattle, what prompted you to come down and challenge it?"

"It's not like that Cuz. I heard about it, now I see it. I'm not trying to buck; as a matter of fact I'm trying to get in. One of the reasons I wanted to holla at you and Lil Bull, I got something you might be interested in."

"You know I'm always in search of something new; shut it down, dish clowns and meet us at Dad's in twenty minutes."

"That sounds like a winner."

"What's on your mind?" I asked Lil Bull, sensing something was bothering him.

"I don't fuck with Cuz, that Nigga is a hoe. Any Nigga that let a Nigga run him out his own Hood got bitch in his pants." He said with a hint of disgust.

"I feel you on that."

The sun was just coming up and the smell of sausage, grits, and eggs filled our nostrils the moment we enter Dad's. "I got a taste for some pancakes." Lil Bull said with a smile."

"You already know what I'm ordering." I shot back, happy to discover his attitude had lightened up. No sooner than we order Salt Rock came through the door just as happy now as he was less than an hour ago. I wanted to laugh when he sat down next to Lil Bull and nudged him slightly to move over some. Refusing to give an inch, Lil Bull placed his elbows on the tables consuming even more space in the small booth. In an attempt to avoid a conflict I ordered the waitress to bring a chair and place it at the edge of the table.

Reluctantly Salt Rock got up and shot Lil Bull an evil look, wondering what he tripping off. "Check this out Cuz." Salt Rock said and slid an envelope across the table.

I retrieved the envelope and was immediately captured by the first of four photographs. After studying it briefly I slid it to Lil Bull who appeared just as drawn. There was nothing more attractive to a gangster than the sight of a cache of automatic weapons. After studying the remainder of the photographs I turned towards Salt Rock.

"I assume they're for sale?" I asked.

"Yes they are." He said and smile.

"How long would it take for you to deliver them?" I continue the probe.

"You can pick them up tonight, if the price is right."

"What's the asking price?"

"It depends on how many you want?"

"I want them all."

Forty thousand dollars was a small amount for twenty- military grades AK-47's and fifteen Clock 9mm. As always Lil Bull was somewhat skeptical, wanting to know more. I never was one to look a gift horse in the mouth. It wasn't no secret we were short on firearms, we were putting in so much work in Southeast, we were shaking hot pieces just as quick as we got them. Only a fool kept a gun with a fresh body on it, and everyone in my crew knew better than that.

I rolled over and stared at the ceiling. I was spent, satisfied beyond measures. Akeelah was the perfect sex partner with the exception of one area, she didn't suck dick; but the magical tricks she did with her pussy over compensated for the lack of head; even so I was determined to get her to do things she never done before. Unlike Felicia or Trisha, whom I had complete dominance over; Akeelah was her own woman, and very much in control of her emotions and her life. As hard as she tried to maintain her independence I was gradually tearing her defenses down;

which was evident by her need to see or speak to me daily. I couldn't deny I enjoyed her company just as much as she enjoyed mines. Sex was just one of many aspects of our relationship, which the majority of our time was spent exchanging meaningful conversation about everything except CCO.

"Are you hungry?" She asked and rolled from the bed.

"Hungry for you;" I said and smiled while admiring her flawless body.

"Boy you need to stop, look at you." She giggled and pointed towards my lion that appeared to be resting peacefully. After trying and failing to wake it up, I reached down and shook it a few times.

"You might have to lick it to wake it up." I continued to shake it.

"Don't you wish?" She said and returned to bed and took me inside her hand and massaged it until it was nice and hard. "This is what you want?" She whispered and climbed on top and guided me inside her. No woman I ever had the pleasure of loving rode a dick the way Akeelah did. I especially loved the way she squatted on top and allowed her inner muscles to massage every inch as she engulfed me with a look of sheer pleasure oozing from her eyes. This was most definitely heaven on earth.

We were scheduled to meet up with Salt Rock in less than an hour. After analyzing every possible scenario Lil Bull and I decided no extra security was required to complete the transaction. Salt Rock would be a fool to cross us, and wouldn't live long enough to spend the money if he did. In route to Naranja Street, which was located in an area known as Little Africa just a few blocks on the outskirt of our Hood Lil Bull and I decided to show up early in an effort to check out the scenery. All appeared quiet as we made a left turn on 54th Street; as a matter of fact shit was too quiet for this neighborhood.

"Did you see that?" I asked Lil Bull as we passed a dark sedan with two Caucasians slumped down in their seat.

"Yeah I saw them." He said and unlocked the power locks on the doors in the event we had to make a fast exit.

6.

"Heads up Cuz," Lil Bull whispered. I spotted two more on Groveland, here they come." I glanced in the rear view mirror and noticed another dark sedan with four occupants riding my bumper. I continued towards Naranja where I made a left turn heading towards Euclid Ave and a better chance at shaking their ass. This big ass Range Rover was not the idea vehicle for a high speed chase, nor was it the type of car you can shake the police for a few blocks and get rid of the contraband. As we proceeded down Naranja and passed the apartment complex we were scheduled to meet Salt Rock we noticed several more agents rushing towards their cars. I decided once we hit Euclid our only chance of surviving was to punch it. Create a little distance and jump out the car and run. The hood was at the bottom of the hill; if a gangster got caught in his own hood it was meant to be.

Concentrating on the cars behind us, I didn't notice law enforcement agents mobilizing a short distance in front of us. Just as I decided to punch it a white Bronco came charging at us. I swirled hard to the right and jumped the curb to avoid a collision.

"Freeze, San Diego Police! Put your fucking hands where I can see them!" Blinded by the lights, I adjusted my eyes and could see the image of a red face, white man hanging out the passenger side window with a 12 gauge leveled at my head. Within seconds we were surrounded by plain clothes officers all wearing yellow wind breakers with Task Force written on them.

"Driver, take your left hand and open the door and step out the vehicle with your hands above your head." I complied with the instruction and was immediately handcuffed and placed in the back of a police car. Lil Bull repeated the process and was placed in a separate car.

After a quick search of my vehicle, the police discovered two firearms and a small bag containing forty thousand dollars in all hundred. I sat in stunned silence as the police rejoice by high fiving and patting each other on the back. The implications were clear; and I felt powerless to stop the next chain of events I was certain would send me back to prison. It was obvious Salt Rock had set us up; why, it really didn't matter. The thought of killing Cuz brought me a brief moment of satisfaction; in the meantime I had something far more important to deal with, like the criminal justice system.

Shortly thereafter Lil Bull and I were transported to the San Diego Police Department and placed in separate holding cages. Despite the fact I was freezing my ass off I didn't complain. It wasn't by accident the temperature was turned all the way down; this was just one of many tools the authorities used to break a man's resistances. I closed my eyes and tried to concentrate on something other than the cold. I tried to recount how many gangsters I killed or drug dealers I robbed since I been home. I stopped counting at thirty-five.

"Anderson!" A voice shouted. I opened my eyes and found Homicide Detective Sullivan standing at the grill gate. It was obvious by the puffiness around his eyes someone awoke him out of his sleep and informed him of my arrest. He beckoned for me to follow him to an interview room.

"Would you care for a cup of coffee?" He asked.

"Yes." I nodded.

"Would you like sugar or cream?"

"Black is fine." I said as I look around the room and noticed several cameras mounted on the wall. Detective Sullivan returned with two cups of coffee and placed one in front of me. I glanced at the cup briefly before I picked it up. The hot liquid felt soothing, like a cup of Brandy on a cold winter night. I could feel Sullivan's eyes on me, studying my every move, wondering what was going on inside my mind."

"Pretty Boy" he said my name like we were close acquaintance. "You know why you're here. You're a suspect in a number of murders and armed robberies, not to mention being a felon in possession of a firearm." He said and eyed me with a blank expression. "Do you have anything to say in your defense?"

"I'll see you in court."

Suspicion was simply not enough to support probable cause for an arrest. Despite his greatest efforts Detective Sullivan didn't have a damn thing to build on. If he thought for a second I would incriminate myself and give him the evidence he needed to prosecute me he was sadly mistaken. I had been in the game long enough to know how the game was played. The number one rule following an arrest, keep your trap shut.

I wasn't a fool to believe my silence meant these charges would simply disappear. Law enforcement had five years from the date to file charges, and more times than not past mistakes had a way of catching up with you in your most vulnerable times. Although incarcerated, I was far from being weak. My money was large enough to mount an effective defense if called for. If that wasn't enough I had a crew of killers on standby, willing and ready to eliminate any witness if one appeared. Never one to sweat shit I had no control over, the day of my arrest my mind was already staging my return.

The Bullshit Never End
Chapter 6

Forty-eight hours minus weekends and national holidays was how long the State of California had to charge you with a crime. It was during this time the District Attorney examined the legality of your arrest. The million dollar question, did the police have probable cause to stop or arrest us? According to the District Attorney's Office they did not.

In an attempt to protect Salt Rock's role as an informant the police claimed they pulled us over because I made a right turn without using my blinker; which was false, but even if it was true, at best I would have been looking at a traffic citation. Instead the police executed a felony stop; when there was no reason to believe a felony had been committed; which made the guns and money inadmissible in a court of law. Even though they were right it didn't excuse the requirement for a 4th Amendment stop. Thank God for the United States Constitution.

We won on a technicality; nevertheless we still had state parole to content with, which went by a lesser form of proof. A Preponderance of Evidence was evidence when weighed against other evidence had a more likelihood of being true. Based on this standard of proof we were dead in the water, which was a mild price to pay for a costly mistake.

Immediately following a DA rejection of our case Lil Bull and I was transferred to the South Bay Detention Center, a facility that had a contract with the California Department of Corrections to house parole violators. Due to the Feds like accommodations and its close proximity to home most parolees tried to delay their revocation hearing as long as possible.

Lil Bull and I were placed in unit 4B where most offenders with extensive criminal records and strong gang ties were housed. Due to overcrowding new arrivals were assigned to the dayroom and placed on a waiting list for an available room. Sleeping in the dayroom was not an idea situation, our first option was to buy someone's room; our second option was to take someone's room. The strong preying on the weak was a long standing practice in every jail; if you can't handle the heat stay out the kitchen.

Fortunately for the two prisoners we keyed in on they agreed to sell their room for a carton of cigarettes. Once we got situated Lil Bull beckoned Eddie Pree to join us. Eddie Pree was an old school hustler three years our senior. I first met Eddie Pree when I was thirteen serving the first of three bids in the California Youth Authority.

After taking a trip down memory lane we moved to a more serious subject, the obvious racial tension that could be felt the moment we walked inside the unit. Eddie informed us racial tension had been building between the Blacks and Mexicans for some time. Based on what he was telling us I was surprised shit lasted this long without the two groups going at it.

Unit 4B like most units in the county jail systems was ran by a tank captain, an assistant, and six workers equally divided by all races. The fact that the tank captain and all the workers were Mexicans suggested they thought very little of the Blacks. The tank captain and his crew control everything from food rations to the distribution of laundry, which on the surface may appear insignificant to a layman, but something worth fighting over for a prisoner. No one enjoyed being oppressed, least of all a gangster.

Realizing a clash was inevitable I pulled a few blacks to the side to get a better feel on their thinking. I was surprised to learn most of them looked forward to a confrontation with the Mexicans. Being a man that's seen more than my share of racial disturbances I understood the rules of engagement that applied in prison could not be utilized in the county jail. In the county jail any assault involving a weapon was grounds for prosecution.

Planning and executing a major demonstration in the county jail was a tricky situation. Even inciting a riot was enough to warrant five more years added onto whatever sentence you already had. With the threat of prosecution as a strong deterrent I convince Lil Bull and Eddie Pree our best plan would be no plan. When the shit hit the fan everybody get a man. Later that evening I had to pull Lil Bull to the side and stress the importance of not having our names linked to a county jail uprising. We already dodged one bullet, why risk catching more time on the front line when we could be just as effective coming from the back field.

It was during a friendly game of poker with Eddie Pree and several Mexicans I learned not all the Mexicans subscribed to the bigotry coming from the tank captain and his homies. Even though some expressed ill-feelings by the way the unit was being run, in the event of a race riot they were obligated to support their people.

Out of all the people I've known in my life I never knew anyone that was remotely as irritable as Lil Bull early in the morning. In jail or on the streets he never responded well when forced to wake up. On this particular morning he asked me to wake him up because he was expecting a visit from his parents. I shook his foot twice; made sure he was up and slipped out the room.

Eddie Pree and I were sitting at the table enjoying our breakfast when Lil Bull emerged. I tapped Eddie Pree on the arm and we both started laughing. Lil Bull had one of the meanest looks a gangster could ask for. The cold part about it; it was a look he could back up in a heartbeat.

"Cuz don't make me clown your ass!" Lil Bull barked at the tank captain. "You got four boxes right there let me get two of them." Lil Bull said referring to the four small boxes of Frosty Flakes Flaco had put to the side for himself.

"I'm not giving you shit homes." Flaco yelled back.

Without another word Lil Bull reached over the cart and took all four boxes. A sudden silence fell over the unit as all waited in anticipation for what was coming next. You could tell by the look in Flaco's eyes he realized he bit off more than he could chew. Win, lose, or draw he had to fight. As Flaco and his homies bailed to his room Lil Bull sat down and offered me two of the boxes in which I happily accepted.

"I think he went to get a knife." Eddie Pree warned.

"I wish he would." Lil Bull said. "That'll give me even more reason to punish his ass." While Pree looked somewhat concern I wasn't worried. I had all the confidence in the world in Lil Bulls ability to handle Flaco, armed or not. I never met anyone that fought harder than Lil Bull, nor have I met anyone that walked away from one of his brawls without assistance. Not only were his hands and feet lethal, his elbows and knees were just as deadly.

Lil Bull was still eating when Flaco emerged from his room with his hand dug deep in his pocket. This was an obvious stunt intended to scare Lil Bull. Flaco motions for Lil Bull to follow him upstairs; he didn't have to ask twice. As Lil Bull stood, so did every black in the unit.

Eddie and I took control of the door immediately after Lil Bull entered the room. No sooner than I shut the door Flaco pulled out a five inch knife fashioned into an icepick and lunged at Lil Bull. Lil Bull took one step backward, timed him perfectly and caught him with a hard kick to his mid-section that sent Flaco sailing into the wall. Like a shark smelling blood Lil Bull moved in catching him with a vicious right hook followed by a left uppercut which laid Flaco out cold. Thirty-five seconds of the first round the fight was over.

I swung the door wide open so the entire unit could see Flaco knocked out. Believing the fight was over all the blacks ran around the unit hooping and cheering and shaking each other's hands. It was a joyous celebration that came to an abrupt end when Flaco's homies pulled out their knives and tried to rush the room trapping Lil Bull, Eddie Pree, and myself in the doorway. Side by side we held our ground by not allowing them to advance. Like a swarm of bees the Blacks attacked from the rear which ignited a full fledge race riot.

By the time the alarm sounded and everyone retreated to their cells there was no one left in the dayroom but the wounded. One by one they were led to the infirmary. In all my years of gang banging I never enjoyed a fight more than the one we just had. It was more like a bar room brawl than a jail house race riot. Besides a few scratches and artificial wounds not one black were seriously wounded.

Unlike state prison where a lock-down normally lasted a month or two, in the county jail a lock-down very seldom lasted longer than a week. I for one enjoyed the solitude of room confinement. It provided me with the serenity I needed to tackle some very important issues; like maintaining control of the Hood and everything I accomplished as a free man.

For the next five days Lil Bull and I spent the majority of our time playing Chess and Dominoes. From the outside looking in a spectator would have assumed we were playing for our life savings when in actuality we were simply playing for bragging rights. As long as I could remember we competed at everything. Because we were so evenly matched the high intensity games only served as an instrument to sharpen our skills.

By the time we came off lock-down I was well rested and ready to deal with the Board of Prison Terms. I was hit and ready to take my lick. All the conversation on earth couldn't talk me out of this one. I was the driver in a car where two loaded firearms and forty-thousand dollars were discovered. Besides that I hadn't reported in over ten months. I was in violation of so many conditions I was fortunate twelve months was the maximum amount of time the Board of Prison Terms was allowed to give per violation.

There was a mixture of joy and wariness looming in the air when we emerged from our cell. Living up to his reputation as a jailhouse politician Eddie Pree summons a meeting between the Blacks and Mexicans. Lil Bull and I remained at the back of the crowd, inconspicuous to the watchful eyes of the deputies in the control booth. With Flaco and his crew out of the picture Eddie Pree nominated himself the new tank captain and promised to run things fair. Without any objections he declared himself the new tank captain and made Looney, a Mexican out of Logan Heights his assistant. Just as he concluded the meeting the sally port door opened and in came a clean cut Mexican looking more like a jar-head than a gang member. By the amount of property he had with him it was fair to assume he was coming from another unit.

"Gentlemen," Deputy Clark announced over the loud speaker. "This is inmate Vargas; he will be the new tank captain; if you have a problem with that too fucking bad."

There was a stunned silence inside the unit, followed by the sound of angry rhetoric. There was no quicker way to unite a unit full of convicts than to violate the Convict Rule of Conduct. Its obvious Vargas was new to the game, because if he wasn't he would have never allowed jail official to put him in such a compromising position.

Eddie Pree and a few other prisoners immediately jammed him up. No sooner than he walked in the unit he walked out; which infuriated Duty Clark. After a brief exchange with inmate Vargas he ordered Eddie Pree to pack all his property and come to the sally port.

"Fuck that shit Cuz; I wouldn't go out there if I was you." Lil Bull yelled.

"Tell them if they want you to bring their asses in here and get you." Someone else shouted. With each rant the coalition grew stronger. Before you knew it Eddie Pree had the entire unit standing behind him.

Hyped up by an overwhelming showing of support Eddie Pree stood his ground. The emergency lock-down alarm sounded for everyone to return to their cells. This was the first of a series of orders everyone ignored. Everything happened so fast, no one had the opportunity to consider the aftermath. We were living in the moment, regardless of the consequences that would follow.

In a daring move to test our resolve over a dozen deputies, in full riot gear entered the sally port like they were about to storm the unit. Instead of backing down we taunted them to come in. "What the fuck are you waiting on; bring your scary asses in here you coward mother fuckers!" Someone shouted. Realizing that we had no intentions of backing down the deputies quickly retreated.

In jail very seldom do you find all races coming together under a common cause. Usually when that happens it's under the most inhumane living conditions. But that was not the case here. In actuality we had no legitimate cause to challenge the establishment in the manner in which we did. We started a fight we didn't have a snowballs chance in hell of winning. What started as a spark, became a bush fire, and in turn became a wild fire that grew out of control. Even if Eddie Pree wanted to stop it he couldn't. It was no longer about him. It was about each individual and their disdain towards authority.

"Gentlemen," a voice came over the loud speaker. "I'm Captain Flores I understand we have a problem. Send a unit rep out and let's see if we can resolve this in a peaceful manner."

Captain Flores threw us a lifeline; and by the expression on everyone's face it was an escape they were looking for. The steam had subsided, and rational minds were back in play. I searched the dayroom for Lil Bull and found him huddled in a group of six. It didn't surprise me when he emerged as the unit rep and proceeded towards the sally port. We

16.

made eye contact and he quickly turned his head. For the life in me I just couldn't understand why he felt the need to be on the frontline.

  Lil Bull returned like he negotiated a peace deal between Israel and Palestine. The look on his face conveyed a silent sense of hope to those that wanted to end this thing in a peaceful manner. Once Lil Bull had everyone's attention he proudly announced jail officials had agreed to all our terms, the most important was the reinstatement of commissary and lost TV privileges that stemmed from the race riot. In return Eddie Pree would be transferred to another unit and wouldn't receive any disciplinary sanctions as a result of this disturbance.

  The power shifted back to Eddie Pree. The revolt started with him, it was only fitting it end with him. Eddie Pree gathered his property, shook a few hands and headed towards the sally port. Shortly thereafter everyone was ordered back to their rooms for a head count. Staying true to their word twenty minutes later the doors were unlocked and we were allowed to shop at the commissary.

  "Cuz what did I tell you!" Lil Bull shouted. "I can look in a man's eyes and tell if he's lying. Cuz the only thing these pigs respect is power. When the Blacks and Mexicans come together who the fuck can stop us?"

  Contrary to what Lil Bull thought I knew better. True enough we would have mounted a defense had they rushed the unit, but after everything was said and done we would have paid a tremendous price. San Diego Sheriff Department was without a doubt the shrewdest and most brutal law enforcement agency in the city. For whatever reason they decided to spare us; and that alone was grounds to celebrate.

  Lil Bull became the new tank captain and the man of the hour. I watched from afar as he retold the story of how he single handily made the deputies bow down and succumb to all our demands. I chuckled as I observed the joyful look in his audience eyes. I was happy Cuz found something to laugh about.

  By the time lock down came Lil Bull was all talked out. Normally we stayed up until 1 am talking about future plans, but as the new tank captain he was obligated to get up at 5 am each morning to prepare the unit for breakfast; which was a task I was sure he would have a hard time fulfilling.

After tossing and turning all night I climbed from the bed and decided to knock down some push-ups until they opened our door for breakfast. No sooner than I completed the first set I heard the sound of the sally port door being open. As I proceeded to the door to see what was going on a deputy appeared at the window.

"You got five minutes to pack all your shit." He shouted and kept moving. I stepped to the window and wasn't surprised when I observed over fifty deputies in full riot gear entering the unit.

"Lil Bull, Lil Bull!" I shouted. "Wake up Cuz it's going down."

"What's going down?" He asked, half sleep, half woke. Before I had a chance to tell him our room door flew open and two deputies stormed inside.

"Look here we got one still in the bed." A big corn fed white deputy said and approached Lil Bull who still hadn't gotten up. "Boy what are you waiting on an invitation, get your black ass out the bed and put your hands on the wall."

"Fuck you, put your hands on the wall punk ass white boy." Lil Bull shouted and jumped up and got right in deputy Bad-Ass face. Lil Bull's sudden move, combined with his size and aggressiveness startles the big corn feed white boy.

The realization that he just got punk right in front of one of his fellow officers was more than Deputy Bad-Ass could stomach. In a blind fury he lunged for Lil Bull's throat. Lil Bull grabbed him by his wrist, side stepped him and drove his elbow in the center of his back. As the other deputy reacted so did I by grabbing him by the back of shirt and ramming him into the wall. What started off as a light two on two scuffles quickly turned into an infamous county jail ass kicking when a swarm of deputies converged on our room and quickly overpowered us? As we fought for dear life the last thing I remember was a powerful grip around my neck. Sleep came quick.

Battered and bruised it was evident by the amount of pain I was in, the deputies continued to beat me while I was unconscious. As I laid face down on the cold dayroom floor with my hands cuffed behind my back I searched for Lil Bull. A short distance away I found him far worse than I. Not only was he beaten severely, the deputies stripped him naked and hog tied him with steel shackles. Unable to look at my rode dog in such a weakened state I turn my head. I couldn't believe these coward mother fuckers were handling my homie like that. All I could think of, if I had a gun I'll kill each and every one of them.

By the time the sun came up all 49 occupants of unit 4B were dressed out and waiting to be transferred. I looked around the holding cage and took note of all the lone faces that seemed surprised that jail officials didn't keep their word. Never in my life have I ever seen a group of men looked so pitiful. It was a miserable sight, one that showed no resemblance of the strong courageous mob that vowed to fight to the end just a few hours ago. What bothered me wasn't the fact jail officials broke their word, because to me their word never meant shit from the start, but the fact that not one person besides Lil Bull and I mustered up enough courage to fight back. I felt like we took an ass kicking for nothing, the type of ass kicking you'll remember for the rest of your life.

Lil Bull and I was transferred to the downtown County Jail, better known as Central Lock-Up, and placed in solitary confinement. A week later I appeared before the Board of Prison Terms and received a year violation. Nine months in on a year I was somewhat surprise when I was sent to New Folsom B-Facility, a maximum security prison to complete my last three months. Here I was back in the midst of some real gangsta shit, on a yard filled with prisoners serving a life sentences. It was an ugly situation that demanded a quick and immediate adjustment. I held no illusion Detective Sullivan was behind my new deployment, and as fate would have it I couldn't have arrived at a worse time.

After conversing with some of my old school CCO partners I learned CCO was on the verge of disbanding. The California Department of Corrections had finally adapted an effective strategy to contain their gang problem; kill the head and the body will die. CCO was already battling internal conflicts amongst its Generals, now with the absence of Tabari, Suma, and Askari whom were isolated in Pelican Bay; in which no one had heard a word from in over a year CCO was on the verge of collapse. After years of constant battle with no ending in sight the mindset of many was to abandon the very oath they once pledged their life to uphold. I remained silent, feeling indifferent to the matter. Unbeknown to the comrades I had made a move a long time ago, and had no intentions of revisiting the past. Talib also informed me there was tension in the air between the Blacks and Mexicans over a handball court which both races claim to have exclusive rights over. I looked around the yard and counted a total of eight handball courts and concluded if it wasn't the handball courts it would be something else. As I made my rounds collecting commissary and supplies from old constituents I noticed Black was laying in the cut to speak to me. I handed Angel from Five-Duce Broadway the two bags of commissary and proceeded towards Black.

"Pretty Boy, how are you doing Cuz?" He asked.

"I'm alright Cuz, how about you?" I asked. Black was Zuberi older brother, and it was on his suggestion Zuberi asked me to handle Lil Man. Unbeknown to Black it was also I that ended his brother's life.

"You know it's a constant fight for life. The day I give up is the day they win. Cuz I wanted to thank you for handling that situation for my brother, you don't find a lot of homies out there that's staying true to the game. He spoke real highly of you the last time he came to visit. Well I see you got your hands full, Cuz if you need anything please don't hesitate to ask."

"Will do, appreciate the offer."

I rejoined Angel and relieve him of one of the commissary bags. Angel and I were the only Crips left in the orientation unit waiting for bed space on the compound, which usually didn't take long because people were constantly going to the SHU for one reason or another.

"Cuz I hope you got some Jolly Ranchers inside one of those bags."

"Cuz whatever is in there you're good to get half." Although I just met Cuz it really didn't matter; he was a Crip like I, and in the same situation as I. Cuz had my back and I had his. It was only right I gave him half of whatever I had. "You feel like shooting these bags inside on the next movement?" I asked as I continued to search the compound for Papa C.

"Yeah, who are you waiting on?"

"Papa C, Cuz went to the commissary to grab me a couple of bags of Taster's Choice."

"Isn't that Cuz right there?" Angel said and pointed towards a group of prisoners coming up the walkway.

"Yeah, that's Cuz." I said, happy I didn't have to wait outside another movement. As we proceeded towards Papa C we heard a scuffle from behind us. Angel and I turned at the same time and spotted two Mexicans stabbing a black. We dropped the bags and rushed to the brother's defense. It was at that moment the entire yard erupted into a full fledge riot. Once again the Southern California Mexicans launched a full scale attack against the Blacks; and once again the Blacks were not prepared to defend themselves. Unlike San Quentin seven years ago the Blacks didn't run and as a result many of them were seriously wounded.

When the smoke cleared six laid dead; five from stab wounds, and one from a single gunshot to his throat; the sad part about it he was also serving a few months on a parole violation, and was also housed in the orientation unit. Scanning the area where his body lie dead I couldn't understand how he managed to get shot. There wasn't a Mexican anywhere in the area. He wasn't attacking anyone, nor was he being attacked. He was just a young brother outside trying to get some fresh air, and now he was dead.

The smell of gun smoke and tear gas lingered in the air. The aftermath resembled a scene from a North and South Civil War movie. While the injured was carted off the yard I searched for Angel and Papa C, and was happy to discover they were okay. I then directed my attention at the Mexicans and noticed every one of them had on white T-shirts with their heads shaved bald. Had you not known them personally it would have been hard distinguishing one from the other. Once again I couldn't do nothing but give them their proper dues for a well-executed move.

Later that night I laid awake thinking about the brother that lost his life. The most disturbing aspect of his death was how easily that could have been me. I now understood why the authorities elevated my custody. At first I thought it was merely to inconvenience me, now I knew better, I was sent to New Folsom B-Facility to die.

Shortly after the midnight count I removed the zipper from my pants and went about the tedious task of cutting a six inch piece of steel from my metal bed frame. I learned years ago steel cuts steel regardless of size or shape. It was a painstaking job, one that left my fingertips numb and bleeding. As painful as it was, it had to be done. I had no doubt whatsoever my brothers would answer the call for vengeance, and like seven years ago I long to be a part of that call.

As fate would have it New Folsom was still on lock-down when I was called for release. I wasn't sad or mad, soldiers came and went but the battle raged on. New Folsom, like San Quentin was an environment of great despair; where the concept of death was more consoling than life. It was a place where bad people became evil, and evil people became lethal. I felt for those that were condemned to a lifetime of hell, especially the young who have yet to live long enough to fully understand the purpose of life. Freedom was the foundation of happiness, and the number one element that separated Man from Animal. Man was not created to live in captivity, but I understood when you act like an animal, society had a right to treat you like one.

Best Man Win
<u>Chapter 7</u>

The hood was alive and prospering, and it appeared everyone was getting money. The most obvious was none other than Lil Joe who had a number of dope houses and a gambling shack on 42nd and Market Street. Every night, from every set, hustlers and players, Crips and Bloods, friends and foes would venture inside the hood and try their luck. As I sat there and listened to the homies vent their frustrations with Lil Joe I recognized immediately they were building a case, one that would justify putting him out of business.

Thus far we had stayed out the lower 40's and allowed 41st Hustlers a free realm to do as they please. I sat back and quietly listened as the homies expressed their own personal reasons for coming at them and decided not to discourage or encourage the talks. In the back of my mind I knew the clock was running, and it was just a matter of time before Joe got his issue. I realize robbing Joe could spark an all-out war between Forty-First Street, and Four-Seven Block, but the threat of war never stopped a gangster from doing what he wanted to do. I studied the faces around me and realized Pope John Paul II couldn't save Joe and his crew from the wrath we were about to release upon them.

The Crime Game was becoming increasing more violent and deadly. The 38 revolver was replaced by the Glock 9 and 45 with longer clips, and the shotgun was replaced by the AK47. We were in the business of kidnap, robbery, and murder; and we were way ahead of the game. Unlike most gangsters you heard about us, but you never seen us.

In spite of a vigorous investigation where law enforcement knocked on every door, interviewed every resident they were baffled not one person had anything bad to say about us. As long as we had the community behind me I knew the skies were the limit.

I couldn't help but admired the way Brenda Edwards carried herself, even in middle school she would stop at the entrance of a door and refuse to enter unless a boy opened it for her. One day I decided to challenge her. When I refused to open the door leading to our classroom she blocked me from entering and we both were cited for being late. "When I asked what she was tripping off? She told me a gentleman always opens the door for a lady." I responded. "I'm not a gentleman, I'm a Crip, and she's not a lady, she's a hood rat." Had I known a brief moment of humor would create a lifelong of disdain I would have chosen my words more wisely?

Unlike most black families in the Hood the Edwards were considered black royalty. Two sons and two daughters that were all considered successful in their own rights; but none more successful than the youngest son City Councilman Byron Edwards, whom was known as the Prince of Southeast, at least until he fell out of grace with the very community that went out of their way to get him elected. Four years ago Byron was a neighborhood celebrity, a local son that defied all odds and made it to City Hall. I, like most residence of Southeast didn't think shit of Byron or his voting records when it came to the welfare of those who really depended on it. Although I never met him I knew his brother Brandon, a wild child in his early years, turned eighteen and joined the armed forces. Last thing I heard he was stationed in Germany. I also knew his sisters Barbara and Brenda, whom I shared several classes with in middle school.

It had been over ten years since I last seen her and twelve years since we last spoke, but I remember her well. I didn't have the slightest clue what she wanted when she showed up at Dad's to speak to me. I stood up and studied her briefly as she approached my table. Jet black and still ugly as a motha fucka, Brenda was blessed with a body that over compensated for her attitude and her looks.

"Ms. Brenda what do I owe the pleasure of your visit?" I smiled and extended my hand. Her refusal to return my smile, followed by a flimsy handshake made it obvious this was anything but a social call. My immediate reaction was to have her ass escorted back where she came from.

"Floyd let's get one thing clear, I don't like you, and I'd rather not be here. For the Lord in me I don't know why my brother, Councilman Byron Williams would like to have a word with you, but he does. He asked me to give you his number, and suggest you call him at 7 pm this evening."

I retrieved the number from her hand and without looking at it tore it up in pieces. "Tell your brother I said the next time he extends an invitation send a more respectable carrier. Now bitch get your monkey looking ass out of here."

"Floyd you haven't changed a bit, I knew it was a mistake coming here." She said and stared at me in utterly disgust. Without another word she wheeled around and headed for the exit.

"Wasn't that Brenda Edwards?" Kenwood asked and took a seat across from me.

"Yeah that was her." I said with a bitter taste in my mouth. There was nothing I despised more than an ill-mannered and disrespectful bitch that was rude for no apparent reason.

"Don't tell me you're fucking, because I have been trying to get some of that pussy since the ninth grade. I use to go to her track meets just to watch her ass jiggle."

"I know what you mean, Brenda use to have a thousand mother fuckers following her to class just to get a glimpse of that ass. To answer your question, no I'm not fucking, not saying I wouldn't put a bag over her head and lay this dick on her."

"What did she want?" He asked curiously, still staring at the exit quietly hoping she would return.

"I don't know; the bitch was so rude I never had a chance to find out."

"I see she hasn't changed a bit." He said and laughed.

"No she hasn't." I joined him in laughter.

Just as the laughter died down our attention was distracted by a clean-cut, all American, G-man coming through the door. It wasn't often you found a young black man in these necks of the woods with no facial hair; that alone represented law enforcement. Mike Loc and Lil Buggs zoomed in on him immediately. The moment they tried to pat him down he took two steps backwards and slid his hand inside the folds of his suit. Okay we get it, you're armed, but can you read, the sign above the door clearly states: No Firearms or Weapons allowed. Absent of a warrant my man was stuck in his tracks, which he quickly acknowledge. After a brief exchange G-man removed his hand from his jacket and walked out the door.

The day was becoming stranger by the moment, first Brenda, now a G-man, what the fuck was going on? Just as I was about to summons Lil Buggs, who, along with Mike Loc was still posted at the entrances G-man reappeared, this time he submitted to a pat down. Mike Loc held him in check while Lil Buggs approached me.

"Cuz would like to speak with you." Lil Buggs said like he was looking for the okay to send him on his way. Dad's was our headquarters; the most secured building in the hood, and the spot we felt the most comfortable. It wasn't every day we had an intruder, and no one, not even I enjoyed when our peace was disturbed."

"What he want?" I asked while keeping my eyes on him.

"He said he needed to speak to you privately."

"Bring him over."

"Have a seat." I said the moment we made eye contact.

"I'd rather stand." He shot back.

"No, I insist, I don't like anyone standing over me. Either you're going to sit or you're going to get the fuck out of here."

"If you insist," he said and reluctantly sat on the edge of the seat.

"What can I do for you?"

"Councilman Byron Edwards is parked outside, and was hoping he could have a few minutes of your time."

"I have no problem with that, tell him I said to come inside."

"He'd rather you join him in the limo, if that's not a problem?"

"It is, tell Byron if he wants to talk come inside, if not keep moving."

"I will relay the message." G-man said and rose from the table. For the most part I've always respected power. Contrary to what Byron thought, whatever degree or position he held in corporate America didn't mean shit here. He was out-of-bounds; a crackhead would have received more love.

I studied him carefully when he entered Dad's with a white button down shirt, and sleeves rolled up. Dark complexion, muscular with Bull hawkish features Byron shared all his family's traits which were clearly a sign of strong genetics. Unlike his sister he knew when to bow down. Upon entering he held his arms outwards and submitted to the most humiliating intrusion of his life. If he had a Tic Tac hidden in the crack of his ass Mike Loc would have found it. Satisfied he wasn't wired Lil Buggs escorted him to my table.

"Byron have a seat, would you care for something to drink?"

"No, I am fine." He said and made eye contact and held it. I don't know what he saw, but whatever it was he obviously decided to change his approach. There was only one King in this establishment and that was me. A smile quickly came across his face and he extended his hand.

"I must say Floyd it's harder to get a one on one with you than it is with the President of the United States." He said jokingly.

"Like the President, I'm a busy man; what's the reason for your visit?" I said on a more serious note. The last thing I wanted was to give Byron the impression this was a social encounter, one that I welcomed. To me he was a nickel slick politician capable of saying whatever he needed to say to get what he wanted.

"Floyd your name has been ringing in the Halls of Justice, and unlike many of my constituents I appreciate everything you have done for the community. I would be the first to admit many of my colleagues had written off Southeast San Diego as a lost cause, a neighborhood not worth saving, but I have always held out hope, refusing to forsaken the very community I grew up in, and which by the way my family still resides. What you started I'd like to build upon, but I need you and the community to stand behind me. As it stands there's no voice stronger than yours in Southeast, a silent endorsement from you, and a strong voter's turn out would more than likely guarantee my reelection; can I count on you?"

"Spoken like a true politician." I said and gave him a round of applause which seemed to irritate him immensely.

"Pardon me if I'm lost on your humor, what seems to be so funny?"

"You, I find it funny as fuck for you to walk in here and think a punch line would erase two years of non-activity on your behalf. Since you've been in office you have been absent and unavailable, and have failed to meet the needs of the people. If anything I'm more inclined to mobilize against you. All bullshit to the side, based on your track record, you tell me, why should I help you?"

"Floyd I'm sure you're aware San Diego is the most conservative city in the State of California. Due to the high crime rate every piece of legislation I tried to introduce was met by staunch opposition. Believe me when I say, I never gave up on the community. Now that the crime rate is down, and my political capital has risen, I'm in a much better position to tend to the needs of the people."

"That sounds good and dandy; but I've never been inclined to put much stock in what comes out of a politician's mouth. Byron I don't know you, I know of you; just as you don't know me, but you know of me. I can't say for certain what I've heard of you is true, but you can bet your last dollar what you've heard of me is only the tip of the iceberg. I'm inclined to help you, but my assistance will come with conditions; and I need not warn you if you don't hold up your end of this arrangement your next reelection will be your last."

"Floyd, that sounds like a threat?"

"No indeed, that's not a threat, it's a promise." I said and met his glaze. Surprisingly he didn't blink or turn his head like a lesser man would. There was nothing else to be said, the implications were clear, but for some strange reason I wasn't convinced Byron took me seriously, which would turn out to be one of the biggest mistakes he made in his young political career. I rose from my seat and shook his hand. "There is no need for us to meet again, I have your number, and I'll be in touch."

"What did that clown want?" Kenwood asked and sat down.

"The Prince of Southeast needs our help. He failed to get 50 percent of the votes to secure his reelection, and now facing a close run-off, he needs us to hit the streets and get the people to come out and vote."

"Imagine that, but what do we get in return?"

"Nothing," I said and smile, "at least not right now."

"I can tell by that look in your eyes, you're up to something."

"You thought I wasn't?" While Byron was concentrating on the moment I was thinking about the future, and the endless possibilities it presented having a politician in my pocket. The birth of a new scheme always gave me a deep sense of satisfaction. There was nothing I enjoyed more than matching wits with a formidable opponent, especially one that honestly believed he held a competitive edge. In his eyes I was nothing more than a thug, a low life hoodlum, someone he could use and dismiss with the wave of his hand. It was time to open a file on Byron, learn all there was to learn about him, his family, friends, his strengths, and most definitely his weaknesses.

The life of a gangster never had a dull moment, or a point where you could simply relax and enjoy the fruits of your labor. The amount of stress associated with the Crime Game was a high you couldn't buy. Not only did you have to worry about law enforcement, you had to keep your enemies in sight; and more importantly you had to keep a constant eye on those closest to you. Whenever a homie or a friend turned on you the odds of survival were slim to none. My mind was intact, but my body was riddled with scars, stitches from slipping. I had two close calls with death, how I managed to survive was a story only God could tell.

———————

In spite of the greatest efforts of three highly qualified private investigators, Doc and Belinda's whereabouts remained a mystery. As I scanned over their reports I was happy to discover Belinda's mother still resided in Chula Vista, but what caught my attention was the report on Cassie, her 20 years old little sister, who according to the report was a high class stripper in Las Vegas. I studied her photos, and couldn't help but admire her sexiness; a spitting image of Belinda, the beauty, the body, but with a flare of youth and innocence. My first inclination was to kill them both, than after careful consideration decided against it. I realized killing Belinda's mother and sister may satisfy my thirst for revenge but would do little to bring Doc and Belinda to the surface. Doc was a dangerous man, not the type of man you want to antagonize, but one that had to be killed. I realized my next shot may be my last shot. I couldn't afford to miss. After a moment of reflection I decided Cassie would be my best bet to lure Belinda and Doc to the surface.

My plate was full, just as quick as I solved one problem, three more popped up. Lil Bull was facing a life sentence and his trial date was quickly approaching. I could tell by the tone in his voice he was worried. He had one witness against him, his top lieutenant, a cat named Smokey from Little Africa, an area on the outskirts of the hood. In an effort to keep him alive, and guarantee his appearance in court the Feds had him in protective custody, in a unit by himself. One thing about the Feds, very seldom did they provide a get out of jail free card; even when a person ratted they still had to do time; ask Sammy the Bull. Losing Lil Bull was equivalent to losing a blood brother, and I simply wasn't going to allow that to happen, even if I had to kill the prosecutor.

And then there was the matter of Salt Rock who fled back to Seattle and returned as if nothing had occurred. Unlike a court of law, on the streets we didn't need probable cause to book you. Mere suspicion was enough to get your life took. Little did he know he was marked for death, and no amount of talk could save his life? Salt Rock returned to the scene with the same ploy; slinging drugs inside a drug free zone, trying to get our attention. Instead of shutting him down this time we allowed him the freedom to defy established law. Unlike the past when we paid him a visit, this time we stayed away and let him do his thing, knowing law enforcement was covering his every move. In spite of their greatest efforts there was nowhere in the Hood they could hide without us seeing them. A student of the game I knew surveillance cost money, and after two weeks with no visible threat, law enforcement suspended their surveillance, and left Salt Rock with a contact number for emergencies.

We owned the streets and the community protected us. Unbeknownst to law enforcement everyone that cooperated with them did so because they were instructed. The day they pulled surveillance was the day we made our move. I was posted in Ms. Grace's house, the same house law enforcement had occupied for three weeks while Salt Rock was slinging crack across the street.

"Floyd there's a fresh pot of coffee brewing, give it about 10 minutes." Ms. Grace said before she headed to church.

"Thank you Mama." I said and gave her a hug.

An hour later Salt Rock pulled up. I watched him closely as he exit his car, and scanned the surrounding area. Satisfied all was good he headed inside and was stopped by Snake, a professional burglar, and one of his best customers. Holding a small bag with a smile brighter than the sun Snake approached him capturing his full attention. Fully relaxed Salt Rock waited in anticipation to get first action on the items Snake was holding. Silently he was hoping it was jewelry or some type of electronics. It wasn't until Snake was up on him that fright and panic set in. Reaching in the bag Snake came out with a 357 magnum. Salt Rock attempted to flee. The first bullet hit him in the back of his head, shattering his skull and killing him instantly. Calm and collected, Snake approached his lifeless body and unloaded five more shots into Salt Rock's body. Salt Rock's body would remain on the sidewalk for the next four hours before a passerby would notice and dial 911. When the authorities arrived several witnesses came forth claiming to have seen a Mexican running north bond on 49th street.

Had Snake not been a dope fiend he would have been an asset to our organization. Smoking weed and moderate drinking was acceptable, but the use of cocaine or heroin was grounds to lose your life. It was common knowledge a dope fiend couldn't be trusted, and eventually would sell you out for a little or nothing. I promised Snake five hundred dollars upfront and a half ounce of heroin when the job was done; instead he received two bullets in his head, and two in his chest.

I was tying up all loose ends, reacting on my first instinct, leaving nothing up for chance. The hood accepted Salt Rock's demise with mixed emotions, not knowing the crimes he committed against the game. The word on the streets; Logan Heights were responsible for killing him, and I saw no need for people to think otherwise. Only Lil Bull and I knew what he did; and only Snake knew I contracted the hit. Dead men can't talk.

Monica
Chapter 8

In the hood money talk and we had plenty of it, which was obvious by the vast number of exotic cars lined-up around Gompers Park. Mercedes, Porches, Jaguars, big body Cadillacs with all the extras; nothing was over the top. Everything we had come from ill-gains, but could be supported by a legitimate business of some sort. Houses, bars, restaurants, stores, if it was located in the hood we owned it. For those that were unwilling to sell we didn't burn them down we shut them down by barring the community from doing business with them; eventually they all submitted.

Gompers Park was in full bloom when Felicia and I pulled up in a drop-top 64 Impala with 16 switches. I bend the corner on Hilltop Street on three wheels captivating everyone's attention, especially the kids who I loved the most. This was a community function, an event we gave every other Sunday; this was our way of giving back. Three barbeque grills were covered with everything from hamburgers to steaks, supported by two bars stocked with every drink one could image, available and free of charge.

No sooner than I stepped out the car I was surrounded by what appeared to be over a hundred kids vying for my attention. Uncle Floyd, Uncle Floyd they all yelled with their hands out knowing I never arrived without a wad of cash to pass out. Felicia handed me a stack of five dollar bills which I handed out, studying the faces of each and every kid. I paid particular attention to the kids that came through the line twice. Eight and nine years old, they were already with the bullshit. Little did they know they were the ones that would keep this gangster shit alive until the end of times?

I broke away and was quickly confronted by the needs of my people. I stood quietly and listened to their concerns; the grandmothers and fathers; the moms and pops; the wives and girlfriends of those incarcerated; those behind on rent, water and lights bills? Just as quick as they stated their concerns I met them with a little extra. If they were behind on their mortgage I bought the house and lowered the payments. If they needed two hundred I gave them four hundred. Little did they know I needed them just as much as they needed me?

Lil Buggs, Tye Stick, Oldie Loc, and Lil Ron laughed as I tried to maneuver my way through the crowd. This was my Don Corleone moment, attending to the needs of the people, which was a requirement that came with being the Boss.

"What the fuck you niggas find so funny?" I asked as I finally made my way to an area that was reserved for members only.

"You my nigga, you look like Peter Pan and Santa Clause all rolled into one." Tye said, and the laughs continued.

"You niggas can laugh if you want. You might see a hustle, but when I look at our people I see our protection. It's a small price to pay for the service they render. In the eyes of law enforcement we're crooks and gangsters, but in the eyes of our society we're Saints and Saviors, we've got to help and protect them at all cost; because without them we'll never survive."

"We hear you nigga." Lil Buggs said and they continued to laugh. Suddenly the laughs came to an abrupt end as everyone's attention were diverted to a drop-top 325i BMW that just pulled up. I turned around to see who they were looking at and observed a beauty that was hard to describe. I don't believe America realizes you can find some of the most beautiful women right in the hood. The average, every day girl who's smile seem to light-up everything around her. It wasn't every day I ran into a woman who took my breath away and made me pause.

"Who is that?" I asked, unable to take my eyes off her.

"That's Monica, G-Loc's sister." Oldie Loc said, and for the first time, in all the years I've known him, displayed some inkling of affection.

"Is she married?" I asked no one in particular.

"No husband, no kids, and no boyfriend;" Oldie Loc added and smiled. It was obvious Oldie Loc was feeling Monica, which was a joy to see. Oldie Loc wasn't the type of Crip that ever exposed his emotions; this was most definitely a rare occasion, and one I was glad to witness.

"Cuz you look like you got a thing for baby girl?" I said in an attempt to learn more.

"Shit who don't?" He said on a more serious note.

"If you feel that way about her why are you still standing here?" I asked.

"Cuz I lost count how many times I tried to get at her. After her brother got killed she refused to give any gangster a moment of her time. The last person she was involved with was that sucker-ass nigga Byron,"

"Councilman Byron Williams?" I asked, cutting him off.

"Yeah, that's the nigga. They were engaged, two weeks before the wedding she shook his ass. I heard she called him out in church, told him to quit lying, and said he had no intentions of helping the community. That was the end of that."

"Okay I can understand sometimes fake niggas play harder than gangsters. Sound like that would have been the perfect time to shoot your stick."

36.

"Cuz what I'm trying to tell you, baby girl don't fuck with gangsters, period."

"Cuz that's what they all say until the right gangster step in their face." I said studying her more closely.

"Cuz you sound like you can fade her?" He said like it was impossible.

"Cuz you must not know my work; nigga there is not a woman on this planet I can't fade."

"Cuz I got five hundred saying you can't fade her." He said, like he was hoping I jumped out there.

"Fuck five hundred, bet a thousand." Lil Buggs interrupted.

"Bet." Oldie Loc shouted and held his fist out. Lil Buggs hit the hammer, the bet was locked in.

In the hood shit moved fast. The word bet was the driving force that separated shit talkers from real gangsters. Put your money where your mouth is; if you said so and someone said different; bet what you believed in.

"A thousand, nigga I got five thousand on my nigga; they haven't made a bitch on this planet Pretty Boy can't fade." Tye Stick shouted.

"She ain't a bitch Cuz." Oldie Loc shot back with a seriousness that took everyone by surprise. My immediate thought was to intervene and squash it before it escalated. Oldie Loc was tripping, which I found puzzling on one hand, and disturbing on the other. Little did he know he was venturing in a danger zone, risking his life behind a woman he never had the pleasure of a kiss.

"Fuck what you're talking about nigga, bet five G's." Tye Stick said and held out his fist.

Once again Oldie Loc hit the hammer, and it was back to business. The spotlight was back on me and my ability to captivate a woman I'd never spoken to a day in my life. Never one to shy away from a challenge I sat my drink down and proceeded towards Monica who was still being flocked by a group of children and adults. The welcoming she received couldn't be matched; the abundance of love was obvious, and unlike me she didn't come with a wad of cash to pass out.

En route I realized she was the same woman Pastor Marvin had spoken about last week when we were discussing building a community resource center in the lot adjacent to his church. My mind was in overdrive searching for the right approach as I closed the distance between us. "Excuse me." I whispered and tapped her on the elbow capturing her attention.

"Hello." She said and smiled, damn near hypnotizing me.

"If you don't mind I like to have a word with you." I said and reached for her hand.

"Sure." She said and gradually pulled her hand away.

"My name is Floyd."

"I know who you are." She shot back and the smile quickly faded from her face.

"By the tone of your voice, and the look in your eyes I get the impression whatever you heard about me is not pleasant?"

"Don't get me wrong Floyd; I love what you're doing around here. You have brought life back to a dying community. You have given hope to the hopeless. Take a look around, I can't remember the last time this park was blessed with so much love and happiness. The people love you, but unlike them I don't believe the end justifies the means."

"If you feel that strongly about it, why are you here?" I said studying her more closely.

"I'm here for the kids, and this just happens to be the only place I can catch them all at the same time. Floyd I'm not naïve to the ways of world, and I believe sometimes God uses bad people to do good things."

"So I'm a bad person, is that what you saying?"

"Are you?" She asked, this time studying me more closely.

"To be honest I don't think so. Just as God uses bad people to do good things, God also uses good people to do bad things. Just as Satan has his soldiers; so does God."

"So you're saying you're a soldier of God?"

"Is that hard to believe?"

"Coming from you, I would say so." She said and giggled.

"I don't know what you find so funny. I find it kind of odd being that we have never met, or spoken a day in our lives and you already condemn me. Are you always this judgmental?"

"No I'm not, and I'm sorry if I offended you."

"Are you really?" I asked, flipping the script.

"Yes I am." She answered and smiled for the second time.

"If you are, and I mean if you're really sorry, allow me to take you to dinner tomorrow evening." I asked and closed the distance between us; and once again she took a few steps backward.

"I don't think so." She said so fast like she was waiting to shoot me down.

"Wow! Never in my life have I ever been insulted and rejected in a single breath. Just as you've read me wrong, I believe I've read you wrong. I truly apologize for wasting your time, food and drinks are on me, hope you enjoy the rest of your afternoon." I said and turned to walk away.

"Floyd," she said my name like she knew me. "I'm sorry you feel that way. Please believe me when I say I don't dislike you; to the contrary I believe you're God sent, just what the community needed. As handsome and intriguing as you are; the fact of the matter is you're a gangster, and I don't date gangsters."

"There you go assuming again; and I'm not talking about being a gangster, because I'm a gangster for real; what I'm talking about is the dating part. I'm not looking for a date; my interest in you is of a business nature. Last week I met with Pastor Marvin and his wife to discuss building a resource center in the lot adjacent to his church. They informed me that you organize most church functions, especially those dealing with the youth and suggested I meet with you to discuss the matter more in depth. When I look around I see our future, and I strongly believe most of these kids have talents that have yet to be explored. Whatever they desire to do with their lives I'd like to make it possible. I'm only one man, and I need help, and I realize the best help will come from those with a personal interest in their welfare. I must admit I was somewhat hesitant in his selection, I was looking for someone much older; but now that I have seen how you interact with the parents and kids; I must agree with Pastor Marvin and his wife, there is no one better qualified than you. For obvious reasons I must take a backseat to this project. I will bankroll it, and build a center that will accommodate the needs of the people. Starting off we will have a budget to cover five instructors, not including the cost of a director, a position Pastor Marvin and I hope you will take. Are you interested?"

"Interested, of course I'm interested. Oh my God I don't believe this. Melba said they wanted to speak to me about a new project, I had no idea they were speaking about a new center." She shouted excitedly and looked in my eyes as if she was seeing me for first time. "Floyd I'm so sorry I misjudged you; I feel so embarrassed, I hope you accept my apology."

"Think nothing of it, apology accepted. Welcome to the team." I said and opened my arms. She slid inside my embrace and gave me a hug like we were long lost friends. Unable to control this strong sensation stirring inside my heart, I released her and took a few steps backward. 'Damn this woman was gorgeous.' I thought and couldn't help but smile. "I have an architect coming by Wednesday afternoon at 2 pm; I would like you to be there if you're available?"

"I wouldn't miss it for anything in the world." She said, and was unable to stop cheesing.

"If I didn't know better I would swear you just won a million dollar jackpot. I have never seen someone so happy."

"Happy I am; this is a wonderful opportunity. You don't know how many years I prayed for God to bless this community with more resources. We have no YMCA's, Boy Clubs, Girl Clubs, or any other community centers for our youth. Heaven knows they need a place to socialize, an alternative to hanging on the block, or at a park with nothing more than a restroom and two cement benches."

"I can feel you on that; and let me be the first to tell you this is only the beginning. Prior to meeting with the architect I'd like to meet with you and explore your thoughts and ideas, which I'm sure you have plenty of."

"Yes I do." She said and giggled, which sounded like a sweet melody, and revealed just how naïve and innocent she really was to my make-up, and the type of man that was standing before her. I wasn't Oldie Loc or the hundreds of other admirers that accepted rejection with a soft heart and became content with a mere smile. I wanted her; perhaps more than I wanted any other woman in quite a long time.

"What does your schedule look like?" I asked, appearing as professional as possible.

"I'm available this evening, if that's not too soon?" She said taking me by surprise.

"This evening it shall be." I said so fast, forgetting it was Felicia's birthday, and I had promised her dinner and a night on the town. "Do you have somewhere in mind?"

"You mentioned dinner, do you like Sushi?"

"Love it."

"Perfect. There's a wonderful Japanese Restaurant in Seaport Village called Taka, I can meet you there at 7 pm."

"Seven it shall be." I said and turned to walk away.

"Floyd." She called out stopping me in my track.

"Yes." I answered not wanting this exchange to end.

"Thank you." She said, unable to conceal her joy.

"No Monica, thank you; you're the Angel, I'm just the tool. See you at seven."

Trapped by a beauty so pure, so captivating I failed to notice Felicia standing quietly in the distance watching my every move. Like a tigress moving in for the kill she was in my face so fast, if looks could kill I would have been dead where I stood.

"Floyd I know you mess with other bitches, but must you do it in my face?" Felicia said as if she was expecting an apology.

"Baby girl don't get this shit twisted, I'm not your boyfriend; I'm your Boss. I do whatever the fuck I want with whomever the fuck I want, have I made myself clear?"

"Yes, you have made yourself clear." She answered and turned her head.

"Glad we understand each other, now get that frown off your face and go get me something to drink. Felicia was my baby, and at that moment the most important women in my life; but like all others she was expendable. Jealousy was a trait that was highly frowned upon and unbeknownst to her, if not controlled could very well dig a hole she couldn't dig out. A smile played across my face as I approached the homies. Tye Stick and Lil Buggs was whooping and hollering like the bet was already over with; while Oldie Loc, like Felicia never appeared more furious. Had I been a bullshit ass nigga I could have claimed victory just based on appearance, even though the deal wasn't sealed. In my life I've been called a lot of things, but fake has never been one of them.

"Cuz you look mad." I said to Oldie Loc, which seemed to infuriate him even more.

"Nigga you ain't did shit, fuck that bitch." He shot back and stared at Monica with a fury fueled by a sick obsession.

"Oh she's a bitch now." Tye Stick shouted. "Nigga five seconds ago you was ready to kill behind her."

"Cuz you got me fucked up. I could give a fuck about her or any other bitch."

"Cuz I'm glad you feel that way; what about that money?" Lil Buggs interrupted.

"Cuz I'm not paying you niggas shit." Oldie Loc shouted and brought all clowning to an end.

"Cuz I don't give a fuck what you're talking about, nigga you're going to pay me." Tye Stick shouted, allowing his anger to overshadow his judgement.

"Nigga I'm not going to pay you shit, now what's happening?" Oldie Loc said and sat his drink down.

"Cuz you niggas are tripping." I interrupted and shot Tye Stick a glance to leave it alone. Gambling and gangsters went hand and hand like guns and bullets. It was understood if you bet and lose you pay; simple as that. I didn't give a fuck if you bet a midget or the mailman, if you lost you paid. Betting on ass or with no intentions of paying was a character flaw that meant you were on some underhanded shit and playing by snake rules.

Oldie Loc was the only member in our crew that wasn't from Four-Seven Block. A straight gangster from Forty-First Street, Oldie Loc had a reputation that made the Hood proud. Recognized as a robber and head banger all rolled in one Oldie Loc shared all the characteristic of a Four–Seven Block Gangster. Although some homies were concerned about his alliance to Lil-Joe, I figured the benefits of recruiting him far outweighed the risk. The ultimate call was mines to make; Cuz was too valuable of an asset to pass up. And besides, if we didn't recruit him there was a strong probability we would have to kill him in the event we did clash with Lil Joe. Fresh out of Donovan Correctional Institution, and like most gangsters, Oldie Loc emerged from prison with a chip on his shoulder and a long list of gangster shit he wanted to undertake. Prison always provided a gangster with the time he needed to plot and plan his return. Unbeknownst to Cuz we were moving on a level he never seen before.

As nightfall shadowed the park and families with small kids begin to depart I searched the crowd for Monica and found her staring back at me. I smiled and she smiled back and waved. I returned her wave and suddenly felt a stab of guilt. It wasn't my style to move in the blind or pursue a woman without an objective in mind. What started off as a game, a young Mack trying to test his hand, had quickly grown into something far more complicated. The mere thought of harboring a square dame for my personal pleasure was troubling. Conditioned by the harsh realities of the crime game I knew what I was thinking, what I was feeling was forbidden. The last thing I needed was a square dame on my line, someone that didn't have a clue about the dangers that existed getting involved with a man like me.

I was glad Felicia's attitude had changed by the time I picked her up in a stretch limo. I think it was finally beginning to dawn on her this illusion she had about us being boyfriend and girlfriend was just that, a young girl fantasy. I was married to the game, bullets and bitches just happened to be a part of it. There wasn't a chick in my life that wasn't expendable, I care about them all until it was time to replace them. Tonight was her night, her wish was my command. Tomorrow it would be back to business.

"You're looking ever so sexy." I eyed her from her head to her pretty toes.

"You don't look too shabby yourself." She reached over and straightens my tie.

"Girl you know I look clean; how many Hood cats you know could rock a 5 thousand dollar Armani suit and look like they ain't ever played in dirt a day in their life.

"Only you Daddy, only you," She smiled and slide her body close to mines. "Thank you Daddy."

"You're quite welcome love. Baby it's me and you until the world end, and when it does I'll meet you in the afterlife, and we'll pick up where we left off."

"You swear?" A small tear fell from her eye; no sooner than I kissed it away another one fell.

"Look at you girl, you're about to ruin your make-up."

"I know, I know." She smiled and started giggling. "I can't help it, I've never been so happy. I love you Pretty Boy."

"I love you too, always have, and always will." I took her inside my arms and felt her body relax under my touch, this was my baby and I was glad to have her on my team.

"Look at me I'm a mess." She said and flipped open her small Gucci purse that was a perfect fit for her make-up kit and a two Dillinger, the perfect weapon when you had to get up close and personal.

"How do I look?" She asked and applied a dab of make-up under her eyes.

"As beautiful as ever," I said and gave her a peck on her lips.

"Daddy I forgot to tell you." She smiled and turned toward me.

"What's up Baby, talk to me."

"Mitch and Alexis came down from Vegas and wanted to hang out with us if that's cool with you?"

"It's your birthday; if it's good with you it's good with me. I heard Mitch was doing it big in Vegas?"

"He is, and he owes it all to you."

'Yes he does,' I thought and concealed my smile.

Had I not been on the look-out for Mitch and Alexis I would not have recognized them the moment they walked inside Benihana's one of my favorite Japanese restaurants. I tapped Felicia on the arm and nodded in their direction. "Mitch, Alexis!" She yelled, waving her napkin. A slight laughter escape my lips, it felt good to see my baby happy. My mind flashed back to the day we met, a young tender and a straight gangster fresh on the scene. The attraction was immediate, but the grooming took time. Out of all the women in my life Felicia was my most trusted companion; she was my creation, the perfect gangsta's chick, vicious on a dick and just as deadly with a pistol.

The last time I seen Mitch he was rocking Hang 10 shirts, Polo's without the pony; now he was all about Versace. I shook his hand and gave Alexis a hug, baby girl was the coolest white chick I knew, a straight Valley girl with red hair and blonde highlights and a few piercing and tattoos that complimented her attitude. I liked her from the moment I met her, she was living her life, doing her, and really didn't care less what anyone thought about it. Like Mitch, her middle school sweetheart Alexis had her own unique style, a free spirit, and living life to the fullest.

I reserved the Chef's Table; a private secluded table reserved for special events. Just as we were being seated the manager asked could another couple in their mid-20 be seated at our table. I glanced at Felicia; she gave the okay which turned out to be a wonderful addition. Paul and Amber were two newlyweds from Canada on their way to Cabo St. Lucas to enjoy their honeymoon. We hit it off instantly, had you not known a passer-by would have thought we had known each other our entire life. Tonight was my kind of night, good food, good wine, and good company. There were plenty of laughs, an abundance of smiles; we were kicking it. After sampling almost every appetizer on the menu we decided to order. Everyone for the exception Felicia and I ordered a steak, Felicia settled for the Hibachi Salmon, and I ordered the Lobster Tails Specialty. One thing I enjoyed about Benihana's the food was so delicious, and no matter how much you ate you never felt stuffed. Time seemed to fly by when we finished the bottle of wine. I nodded at the waiter and twirled my finger indicating put everything on one check. When she returned, Mitch intercepted the check, took a peep and placed eight C-notes in the folds and told her to keep the change. Radiate

The night was still young, feeling and not wanting the night to end we invited Paul and Amber to hang out with us, they gladly accepted. Everyone piled inside the limo and I instructed my driver to head up Pacific Coast Highway where they had a wide range of exclusive night clubs that catered to the movers and shakers of Southern California. Down here money played with money, and there wasn't a better vibes than an environment occupied with successful socialites.

"I come bearing gifts my friends." Mitch said and removed a small gold case from his pocket. "Yummy, yummy," Alexis smiled and started licking her lips when Mitch opened the case revealing a cache of small yellow pills in the shape of a dove.

"What's that?" I asked, clueless.

"Ecstasy my man; the best in the country," He said and swallowed one. "Give me, give me," Alexis shouted like a happy child that couldn't wait her turn. She opened her mouth and allowed Mitch to place one on top of her long, snakelike tongue. Her tongue rolled around the pill twice before disappearing back inside her mouth. Damn I thought, Alexis looked like she'll eat a dick up. "What about you Pretty Boy?" Mitch asked and extended the case. "No I'm cool baby boy." I respectfully declined.

"What about the birthday girl? I don't even know why I asked you." He turned towards Felicia who appeared to be stuck between a rock and a hard place. "Can I Daddy?" She pleaded, hoping I didn't say no. It was obvious by her reaction she tabbed before, and by the expression on her face she couldn't wait to do it again. I thought I knew everything about, it was obvious I didn't. I smiled and nodded, giving her my approval. Tonight was her night, the conversation would come later. Fucking with drugs was taboo, weed was cool, cocaine or heroin will get you killed. Up until now popping pills was a white thing, but ecstasy was starting to cross racial line. Paul and Amber looked like they stumbled across a gold mine. A free dinner followed by some Ecstasy and Lord knows what else?

I sat back and witness their cheers switch gears, and their smiles get wider while their laughter's grew louder. Sheer happiness was always accompanied with a tad of silliness; the only thing missing was some music which Alexis quickly corrected. The Bose Platinum One delivered a surround sound that had them bumping in their seats. Although I was nowhere near the level they were on I was still caught up in the moment. By the time we arrived at the first club everyone was chilling so hard no one wanted to go in. I instructed the driver to cruise up and down the coastline. Once we were back in traffic I turned towards Mitch and told him to give me one.

It didn't take long for me to catch up, the visual hit me immediately. Everything and everyone became colorful. Suddenly I felt light headed, cheerful, and extremely happy. I was on another level, one that made my thoughts so clear, my understanding so deep, and my awareness so complete. Life was so beautiful, if I could only freeze this moment I would enjoy it for eternity.

"Thank you Daddy, this is the best birthday I ever had." Felicia said and slid into my arms and started kissing me.

"I'm glad you're happy baby." I whispered and started kissing her back. Her lips tasted sweet and her body felt so natural against mines. "I love you Daddy." She smiled and allowed a stream of tears to fall from her eyes.

"I love you too baby." I said and meant every word; Felicia was my baby and I wanted everyone to know it.

"That's so cute." Amber said and moved next to Felicia and gave her a hug. The next thing you know Alexis was giving her a hug. "Where is my hug?" Mitch said and joined them. "I want a hug too Paul said. I sat back and enjoyed how silly they all looked. I tapped Mitch to get his attention and bust out laughing. My man had the biggest ears I have ever seen in my life. "I bet you don't miss much, huh Mitch?"

"What do you mean Pretty Boy?" He asked without a clue.

"I mean them big ass ears; I bet you could hear astronauts talking on the moon." The limo erupted in a laughter so loud it felt like the car was shaking.

"I know you didn't." Mitch said between laughs. "I know you didn't." Four hours later we all took another tab of ecstasy and made a camp fire on the beach. We had about 6 more hours of darkness, and planned to enjoy every second of it.

The following evening Felicia invited Mitch and Alexis over for cocktails. Mitch wanted to talk, and I wanted to listen. Every conversation we ever shared a substantial amount of money changed hands. As dorkey as he appeared he had a knack for getting paid.

"Pretty Boy I need your help. I got myself in a jam." He said, and paused. "You ever heard of Dice, a North Side Crip from Vegas?"

48.

"Name sound familiar why?" I lied. I knew Dice well. Dice was originally from West Side 30's, another Crip like Salt Rock who Zuberi ran out his own hood. Taking the skills and knowledge he picked up in Dago Dice went to Vegas and started his own mob. His name was in air and every day he was growing stronger.

"Remember a few months back when you loaned me a hundred G's, well I also borrowed a hundred G's from Dice. I overestimated the Grand Opening and first month profits from Club Nuevo and was only able to pay you. Dice told me don't worry about it and gave me another week to pay him the rest, which I did. As soon as I paid him he taxed me an additional fifty thousand for late fees and gave me two weeks to come up with it. I paid him off in a week. Now I can't get rid of him. Every weekend him and his homies come in the club, take over the VIP section and run the bar tab into the thousands, and refuse to pay. Pretty Boy I really think he's about to make a move on my club, and I don't know how to stop him."

"Alright what you need from me?"

"I need you to get him out of my life. I don't care how much it cost, two hundred thousand, three hundred thousand, you name it and you got it."

"How long have you known Dice?" I asked.

"A little over three years, until recently I thought we were friends."

"How did you meet?"

"I have been serving him and his people weed for the longest. To be honest they are my best customers, they spend at least fifty thousand a month; and that's not counting ten thousand a month on Ecstasy."

"What kind of deal you been cutting them?"

"Not much, instead of charging them $600.00 an ounce for some Cali Green, I charged them $500.00 an ounce. And like everyone else I charged them $25 a tab, no matter how many they buy."

"Damn Mitch you been charging the shit of them; I see why Dice is trying to dig in your pockets."

"No, not really; that's chump change to them. Dice got the Coke game on lock; and besides I been helping them in other ways. Imagine getting paid twenty thousand in all one dollar bills. Dice thinks my club is so popular because I got the best Weed and Ecstasy; what he doesn't know is I was turning out numbers like these when I was hosting underground Raves. People come to my place because I'm one of the closest DJ's in the country. A year ago I was passing out fliers, giving parties in the desert, abandon warehouses with a 4 days' notice trying to stay ahead of the police. I came too far to let Dice take my dream. Pretty Boy you're my only hope, bro you got to help me."

"From the way things sound Dice is about to make a move on you any moment. Don't trip, I got this. First thing I want you to do is close down for a week, when you open back up; you'll be doing it with my people. I'll loan you my bartenders and bouncers from Dad's and also send a few homies to handle security. I wish you would have gotten at me earlier; it would have been a lot easier to handle. You fucked up when you allowed Dice to get a foot in, now we got to nudged him out and try to avoid a war and destroying your club at the same time. Normally I wouldn't get involved in something this risky, but being you're just like family I can't sit by and watch harm come your way. In the meantime I will need you to fall all the way back, and give the appearance the club is under new management. Once we get a handle on the situation we'll gradually move my people out and your people back in; by then Dice should no longer be a problem."

"That sounds like a plan; a peaceful approach that I hope will prevent anyone from getting hurt." He said thoughtfully as he tried to envision my next move.

"I don't want you to hold onto false hope. There is also the possibility this might get ugly. Taking something from you is one thing, trying to take something from me will draw a far different response? Before we can make a move I'll need two hundred thousand up front."

"I'll have the money in your hands by this time tomorrow." No sooner than we shook hands to seal the deal the plot to take it all begin to take form. If Dice had his eyes on it, it most definitely was worth taking a look at. Had he made his move already I would have never got involved. A true gangster will fight to the grave to protect something he took.

Mitch was the Underground King; one of the coldest DJ's in the country. My man had a following way before they invented the product. He was ahead of the game; but the game was catching up, flipping quicker than money could change hands. The feds were giving Crackheads more time than Kingpins. An ounce of Good Cali Weed cost more than an ounce of Coke, and the demands for Weed and Ecstasy far exceeded Mitch's supply. Mitch had the connections he just didn't have the capital or the muscles to make it happen.

Lethal
Chapter 9

I first met Albert Kahn at the neighborhood recreational center hosting a 3 on 3 basketball tournament. Although he was a weekend regular no one paid particular attention to the old white man well into his 60's, who spoke broken English and always sat at the top of the bleachers and cheered for both side. After a while he fitted right in, and became a gym favorite. Albert, like most elders understood the quickest way to a child's heart was to give something free. I couldn't do anything but respect a man that had a child's best interest at heart; it was hard to lose when you bet on a child. Every Tuesday and Thursday he taught a self-defense class free of charge to anyone that arrived. It was his belief if every child knew self-defense they would less likely grab a gun to settle a dispute. Being that we both had the kid's best interest at heart it was just the matter of time before we had a meeting of the minds. That was two years ago and we grew as close as ever.

Albert was an ole Israeli Vet, moved to the states with his wife 12 years ago; since then she passed. Albert and I quickly became friends, followed by student and teacher, and mentor. No one but Albert and I understood our connection. His eyes seen more in a year then most men would see in a lifetime. Although he was one of the most easy-going regulars at the Rec Center I was probably his only friend. Sometimes we would talk or play backgammon for hours; I especially enjoyed when he took out his photo album, and gave me a photogenic glimpse down memory lane. I would pause at every picture, fascinated by the history. It only took a glance for me realize Albert has seen his fair share of killing on God's green Earth. Killing for country was far more rewarding than killing for one's Hood.

Just as much as I enjoyed the lessons in history what I look forward to the most was Sunday and Wednesday when he trained me Krav Maga, a deadly form of martial art that concentrated on close quarters, hand to hand combat. The skills I learned in Albert's basement gave me the tools I needed to disarm and kill in one swift motion. As vicious as I was with my hands and feet I kept it to myself, I never divulged it to no one. Although I had much love for my entire crew, experience taught me sometimes today's friends sometimes turns out to be tomorrow's enemies.

I always ended my training with an hour on the treadmill, followed by an hour on the bag. I arrived home and still had energy. Sunday was a day I reserved for myself; a day I wasn't bothered unless it was an extreme emergency. The evening was just starting and there wasn't anyone besides Monica that I wanted to share it with. I couldn't deny it; I was feeling Baby in more ways than one. The more time I spent around her the more enjoyment I received. She was the perfect fit, the balance I needed to give my mind a rest. No sooner than I reached for the phone it rang one time.

"Hello." She said.

"Monica?" I said and couldn't believe our timing. She was calling me the exact moment I'm about to call her.

"Floyd I hope I'm not disturbing you."

"Baby you could never disturb me; I'll wake-up out of my sleep to get in your ear."

"I got it like that?" She asked, gleaming on the other end.

"You most certainly do." I came back so quick it didn't leave any room for doubt.

"I'm glad, because we've been over here talking about you for the last hour. She confessed with a light laughter.

"Were you? I hope it was pleasant."

"Yes it was. I think my mother is one of your greatest supporters, which I find hard to believe, being that she never met you. All she talks about is you and the wonderful job you have done restoring the peace to our community."

"A mother's intuition should never to be questioned; I'm a firm believer a mother knows best."

"If you say so," she giggled.

"Yes I do, and I would love to meet her."

"I'm glad, because she would love to meet you."

"You name the place and time and I promise to be there. Does your mother cook?"

"Like every day, as a matter of fact she's cooking right now."

"You've got my curiosity running wild, what is she cooking?" I asked, searching for a way to prolong the conversation.

"My favorite, smothered pork chops and rice, sweet corn and peas, hot water cornbread and potato salad."

"You've got my mouth watering, I can't remember the last time I had a home cooked meal."

"That's kind of hard to believe, considering all the female admirers you must have."

"Looks can be deceiving, and I must say I get a lot of credit for things that are simply not true. I'm a single man, who for the most part has dedicated my life to public service. There is nothing I find more rewarding, or more demanding than tending to the needs of the people; it simply does not provide much time to socialize."

"I know exactly what you mean; but some way, somehow we must find time for ourselves. Have you had dinner?"

"No I haven't, I was about to order Chinese food."

"If you're not too busy you can join us for dinner if you'd like? Every Sunday my family comes together at my Mother's house for dinner and conversation. For the past few months you have been the topic of dinner conversation. We would love for you to join us."

"And I would love to join you. Does your mother still live on Hilltop?"

"Yes she does."

"I'll be there in thirty minutes." I hung up the phone and reminisce on the last time I visited her mother's home. It was eleven years ago, and on orders from Doc we lured G-Loc into the coldness of the night and gunned him down for suspicion of snitching; only later to learn it wasn't him but someone else. Looking back it was one of my many regrets. I was sixteen, a young soldier following orders; and at a time when an order was never to be questioned.

The night was still young when I pulled up in front of the Ramsey's residence. I removed the safety on my 9mm and did a quick visual scan of the area before I exit my vehicle. I paused for a moment and felt an overwhelming sense of joy when I noticed an elderly couple standing in front of their homes sharing a laugh. Although everything appeared peaceful and quiet I couldn't ignore the fact that Southeast would always present some element of danger.

The smooth melody of Al Green 'Let's Stay Together' followed by small chatter and the sweet sound of laughter flowed through the living room window. I paused for a moment to savor the sound of happiness, and couldn't help but acknowledge the purity and joy that could only be found in the presence of close family and friends. I waited patiently for the song to end before I finally knocked bringing the laughter to a quiet but curious end.

"Floyd when you said thirty minutes, you really meant it." Monica said and greeted me with a warm, friendly hug.

"I believe a man is measured by his word, and I hate to keep people waiting."

"That's nice to know, please come in and meet my family."

I stepped in the living room and was greeted by four women, all appearing to be professional in their own right. "Floyd this is my sister Michelle." She said referring to a woman in her mid-30's dressed in business attire that shared neither her beauty nor physical attributes. "Hello Floyd." She said and extended her hand. "Hello Michelle, it's nice to meet you." I said and shook her hand. "This is my Auntie Rose." She said referring to a much older woman dressed in nurse attire. "Hello Floyd." She said and also extended her hand. "Hello Mrs. Rose, nice to meet you." I accepted her introduction and returned her handshake. "And this is my Auntie Janis, who you probably remember, because she remembers you." She said and giggles. "I could never forget my favorite 7th grade teacher who taught me the importance of math. Hello Mrs. Green, it's nothing less than a sheer joy to see you again." I said and smiled. "Hello Floyd, it's wonderful to see you again, and I must say I wasn't surprised when I learned you were the architect behind this wonderful movement sweeping across our community, thank you." She said and gave me a hug. I returned her embrace, which was filled with so much love I felt a warm sensation travel through my body. It was at that moment I realized how many lives were affected by the violence the homies had inflicted on the very community we vowed to protect. A brief moment of appreciation passed as I felt all eyes on me. "And you must be Mama." I said and turned towards a beautiful elder black woman with a speckle of gray and appeared to have a grace about her that seemed to command the attention of a Queen. "Floyd it's a pleasure to meet you, welcome to my home." She said and also gave me a hug. "The pleasure is mines, and thank you for inviting me. Monica tells me you're a wonderful cook; I hope I'm not too late."

Dinner couldn't have been more pleasant, never in my life have I ever felt more comfortable in the presence of people I just met. It was obvious by the way they interact this was a close knit family with an abundance of love and admiration for each other. Periodically I noticed each of them staring at me in a quiet curious manner as I tended to the huge meal in front of me. Nevertheless I was happy to discover in the eyes of my community I wasn't the monster that law enforcement painted me out to be. I was a soldier of a different kind; instead of risking my life and killing in the jungles of Vietnam, for a country that neither accepted nor respected me; I was killing on the streets of southeast for the betterment of my people.

"You have a beautiful family." I said, finally finding a moment alone.

"Yes they are amazing, and I won't trade them for anything in the world." She said proudly.

"I'm envious; you're a lucky woman to be surrounded by so much love; it's priceless."

"I really never thought of it that way; thank you for the reflection. What about you? If you don't mind me asking do you have a close relationship with your family?"

"Yes I do; but unlike you my family reside 25 hundred miles away in New Orleans. I'm lucky if I see them three times a year."

"Sorry to hear that, you must miss them dearly."

"I do; but for the moment I find a great deal of satisfaction in my extended family, the people of my community. To them I'm a son, a father, a brother, a nephew, and an uncle. What more can I ask for?"

"Floyd I'd like to apologize; little do you know I was your biggest critic at the supper table. During the past few months, despite the overwhelming support you received from my family I tried my hardest to impeach your character. After meeting and talking with you I can see how wrong I've been. When I look in your eyes I know in my heart you care; and whatever I can to help you all you have to do is ask."

"Thank you that carries a lot of weight with me; and just as you I must also apologize. When Pastor Marvin and his wife recommended you to oversee the community center I was somewhat concerned by your age. Without ever meeting you I naturally assumed twenty-four years of living could not produce the type of experience needed to oversee a project of this magnitude. The stakes are high; the lives and welfare of an entire community hangs in the balance, it's essentials we get this right the first time. After watching you interact with the people, and observing the abundance of love, respect, and admiration they greeted you with, I must admit there is no one better qualified than you to care for their needs. Well it's getting late, and as much as I'd love to prolong this evening I have a full schedule lined up tomorrow."

"Thank you for coming; and before you leave I was wondering have you made any plans for the 4th of July?"

"No I haven't."

""My friends and I are having a poolside barbeque at my place; I would love it if you'd join us."

"I wouldn't miss it for anything in the world."

Tying up loose Ends
Chapter 10

Lil Bull was scheduled to start trial the following Monday; a trial in which things didn't look good at all. The Feds had offered him a plea deal for 30 years; with the threat if he went to trial and lost he would never see the streets again. It was on my advice he turned it down and put his fate in my hands. Thirty years was tantamount to a life sentence; only a visionary could see twenty-four years into the future, which was exactly how much time he would have to serve before he was eligible for release. I had one shot at Smokey, it was imperative I didn't miss; Lil Bull's life depended on it.

Smokey was the only inmate housed on the 5th floor of the Metropolitan Correctional Center, the Feds version of the county jail. The Star Witness and Confidential Informant in twenty-five high profile cases, the Feds wasn't taking any chances with his safety. Tightly guarded and under the watchful eye of the toughest correctional officers, Smokey never left the confines of his unit without at least four escorts; making it absolutely impossible to launch an effective hit; and anything less than killing him was a waste of time. I had a plan, and if everything went according to plan by Monday morning Smokey would be a dead man.

As a child Smokey was a troubled child struggling in a troubled world. A ward of the court since the age of three; and a product of one foster home after another Smokey found his first true family with the East Side Rollin 40's Crip Gang; where Lil Bull took him under his wing and groomed him like a little brother. Despite being 6 feet 6 and 320 pounds Smokey was considered a big ass boggy bear, soft as a box of tissue; that was until the homie June grabbed Suzy's ass and dared her to tell Smokey, which was exactly what she did. By the time the homies got Smokey off June's ass, June was no longer among the living. I witnessed many murders in my life, but none of them compared to seeing a man get beat to death. Some of the homies wanted Smokey's head, but Lil Bull wasn't having it. Now that all was said and done I wondered did Lil Bull have any regrets saving his life.

Unlike the majority of my homies I understood the power and danger of love. The life of a gangster didn't provide room for love and drugs, which were equally dangerous and deadly. It's wasn't a secret Smokey loved Suzy and his four year old twin daughters more than he loved himself or any oath he pledged to Lil Bull or the East Side Rollin 40's Crip Gang. I wasn't surprised when I learned Smokey had flipped the script and joined forces with the Feds. The thought of spending the rest of his natural life behind bars was mild when compared to the possibility of never seeing his wife and daughters ever again. I had to give the Feds their proper dues; they knew exactly who to target to bring down Lil Bull and every other heavy weight drug dealer in the city. As brilliant as their plan, they overlooked one important factor. They did right by protecting Smokey; but at the same time they should have protected Suzy and his kids. Bear in mind we have never held a family accountable for sins of the father; but drastic times called for drastic measures.

"Go get her." I told Felicia and rolled down my ski mask and signal for Mike Loc to kill the lights. Still blindfolded and gagged Felicia led her to the only chair at the table and removed her blindfold. Unaware how many people were in the room I reached over her shoulder pressed play on the small digital screen. Suzy sat frozen, unable to talk, all she could do was watch the video of her 75 years old mother, her six year old nephew by her deceased brother, and of course her 4 year old twin daughters tied up and blind folded.

"Do you love them?" I whispered in her ear. Yes she nodded unable to control the tears rolling down her face.

"Would you do everything in your powers to save their lives?" Yes, she continued to nod her head up and down.

"Even if you had to die so they could live?" She continued to nodded, this time more vigorous than the time before. I believed her.

"Fortunate for you and them, you don't have to die, kids need a mother, but they can live without a father. Suzy your family's lives rest in your hands, just like you convinced Smokey to rat on his people, for your family sake you better convince him to commit suicide. I'm ma release you shortly so you can make the 8 pm visit. If Smokey is still alive come 6 am tomorrow morning your entire family will be dead by 7 am. Do you understand me?" This time she didn't nod, a second flood of tears was all the confirmation I needed. An hour later Suzy was dropped off less than a block away from her home. I couldn't imagine what was going through her mind, nor did I give a fuck. She had two hours to convince Smokey to kill himself, and he had six hours to do it.

Never one to sweat shit I no longer had control over, I returned to Akeelah's to await the outcome. Akeelah always provided a moment of solitude when I needed it the most. She knew when to talk or merely listen; she knew when I needed company or some space to be alone; she knew when I needed that raw, animalistic, high intensity sex, or an intimate touching, slow passionate love making. On the surface everything looked good, but underneath there was something about her that made kept my defenses up. Perhaps it was her ties to Tabari and CCO, or her intellect, or my inability to control her in the same manner I controlled all women in my life; whatever it was she had my senses on full alert.

Akeelah was sound asleep when I arrived home, looking as beautiful as ever. I lean over the bed and gave her a soft kiss on her lips; just as I rose she reached out and grabbed my hand and pulled me on top of her. Our lips met again, this time for a long deep passionate kiss. I loved the taste of her lips and the way our tongues danced around each other.

"What time is it darling?" She licked her lips and laid her head on my chest.

"It's a little after ten o/clock, what time did you go to bed?" I asked and ran my fingers through the back of her hair and softly messaged her neck.

"About an hour ago, I didn't think you would be back so soon; are you hungry? I made some baked chicken and pasta."

"Yes, I'm famished."

"Would you like to eat in here or the dining room?" She asked and rolled from the bed exposing a beautiful tone body, which resulted from eating healthy and exercising five times a week. Had it not been for a few speckles of gray, and a few lines under her eyes it would have been hard to imagine Akeelah was three weeks away from her 47th birthday.

"I'm going to take a quick shower and I'll meet you in the dining room." Akeelah didn't have a clue of the events transpiring in my life. It wasn't that I didn't trust her; there was simply no need for her to know anything that she wasn't involved in. Although I haven't been sleep in over two days I wasn't the least bit tired. Too much was on the line; sleep would have to wait. After flipping it every which way I could I was confident I covered all the bases. Killing came natural, and in most instances it only requires pulling the trigger, which was easy; but trying to convince someone to commit suicide was entirely a different challenge. I didn't know Smokey personally, but the love he felt for his family was no secret. It was this love I was banking on; and in the event he didn't uphold his end, everyone he held near and dear to his heart wouldn't live to see another day.

It was close to 1 am when I emerged from the shower, and I figured Smokey had at least 3 hours to contemplate the task at hand. Silently I wondered if I was faced with the same dilemma how would I react. It was an easy question that didn't require much thought. I would go gracefully; for I didn't love this world, I loved the people that cultivated it.

"Baby what's wrong?" Akeelah asked, snapping me back to reality.

"Nothing; why do you ask?"

"For one Floyd you have been sitting there for over 15 minutes and you have barely touched your food?"

"I'm hungry for you; bring your sexy ass over here." I smiled and opened my arms, allowing Akeelah to wrap her arms around my neck and place her full weight on my lap.

"Floyd I don't know why you feel you can't trust me; like your life must be a secret. You'll never know if I can help you unless you tell me what's going on. You know two minds are better than one. Does this have anything to do with Lil Bull?"

"Here you go again, why you insist on meddling in affairs that you have nothing to do with. How many times must I tell you if you need to know I'll let you know?" I released my embrace from around her mid-section and gave her a slight nudge to get up, in which she quickly did.

"Floyd sometimes you can be the coldest creature on the planet; I hate when you act like this."

"If that's the case quit asking me stupid shit." I snapped as I begun to feel the first stage of fatigue.

"Fine, I won't then. I'm going back to bed." She said and stormed from the room.

I trusted Akeelah like I trusted everyone else, to a certain extent. It was obvious after a year she still didn't understand me or the way I played the game. When it came to business it was mind over matter, regardless how much I was digging a woman, I played them the way a gangster is supposed to play them, at a distance. There was nothing I despised more than a woman trying to question me, trying to pry in shit that didn't concern her. She knew the rules of the game up front, and her constant effort to change them was beginning to make me wonder about her.

The reality of the matter was, Akeelah was the least of my concerns. I had so much shit on my plate a chick was like a traffic ticket in a sea of capital offenses. I glance at the wall clock, it was a little pass 2 am; count time was at 3 am, at which time they should discover his body if indeed he took care of his business. Unlike the Downtown County Jail where we had four guards on the pay-roll, the guards at the Metropolitan Correctional Center were far harder to compromise. Unable to secure a correctional officer we keyed in on Gloria Bennett, a switch board operator at MCC, and the sister of the homie Carlos who was serving Life without the Possibility of Parole for killing a Police Officer and his dog. I was somewhat hesitant about using Gloria out of fear we might have to kill her if she showed any signs of weakness. The rules of the Game dictated we got permission from Carlos prior to approaching his sister for any reason, even romancing. I respected Cuz to the fullest; but this was one of those occasions I couldn't afford to wake him up, let alone secure his permission. It was Gloria or no one, and regardless of what it took, whether by fear, force, or the power of the dollar her cooperation was a must. Much to my relief it took neither. Upon learning what I needed, she gladly offered her assistance. Unbeknownst to me there wasn't a soul in Southeast that didn't believe I was God sent, appointed by the good Lord to restore peace and harmony to a dire community suffering at the hands of Satan's most powerful, addicted, and deadly curse; Crack cocaine.

Time seemed to travel at a snail's pace, as a thousand thoughts raced inside my head. There was nothing else I could do, but wait. It was all or nothing, there was no consolation prize, the stakes couldn't get any higher; freedom versus life in prison. Confident I did all I could do, I sat on the patio savoring the very best of freedom, a strong cool breeze and a pretty blue sky filled with stars. It was exactly 4 am when my cell phone interrupted the moment. I stared at it briefly and after the 4th ring it went silent. No sooner than I picked it up it rung again; this time I let it ring five times before I answered it and placed the receiver to my ear. The voice on the other end was soft, low and clear. I quietly listened, hanging on every word until the phone went dead. I sat back, closed my eyes and felt the weight of the world lift from my shoulders.

At approximately 3:05 am the emergency alarm sounded, followed by a code 4 which required all medical personnel to report immediately to Unit 5. At approximately 3:16 am Smokey was transferred to an ambulance and rushed to Mercy Hospital. At approximately 3:43 am the gangster formerly known as Smokey was pronounce dead on arrival.

Defying all Odds
Chapter 11

All hell broke loose Monday morning inside Honorable Leslie Ann Gallagher's courtroom. Lil Bull, along with 2 other defendants was dressed out and ready for trial; they were the only three left out of San Diego's top 25 most dangerous drug dealers; the other 22 had pled out to astronomical years, which was a decision they will live to regret. Everything was riding on Lawrence Jamison aka Smokey, whom up to this point was a no show. Despite overwhelming objections from the defense, Honorable Gallagher granted the prosecution a 21 days postponement to consider this latest turn of events. There was a mixture of bewilderment and jubilant floating in the atmosphere; it was obvious the prosecutor had a serious problem on his hands.

After riding out the most intense year of his life, the last thing Lil Bull wanted was to lay in the cut. Incarceration always provided a man with much needed time to collect his thoughts and correct reckless behavior. I anticipated the Feds would launch a full scale investigation into Smokey's suicide. I instructed Suzy to tell them she told Smokey she was leaving him because she didn't want to live in fear for her kids. I was confident Suzy would uphold her end; she witnessed firsthand how easy we snatched her entire family without anyone knowing they were gone.

I've always been a man that respected power and understood my place among the powers to be; and any fool that believed he was too big, too fast, and too smooth for the Feds was as dumb as they came. The United States Government will hunt you down; Dead or Alive. The world isn't big enough to hide, they'll go to the ends of the Earth and snatch your President out the bed and gun him down. I couldn't do nothing but respect that.

The time was ripe, we got as big as we could get in San Diego, and it was time to expand. My sights were set on Las Vegas for several reasons; most importantly it was time to resolve old matters, we had one lead on Doc, and it was imperative we didn't miss. There was nothing on this earth I wanted more than Doc and his bitch dead. This was a serious game, which was evident by a body riddled with scars. Graduation came with a cost, I couldn't complain, I delivered it just as vicious as I received it; "Do or Die; Kill or be killed" was the code in which I lived my life. I loved life like the next gangster, but I didn't give a fuck about dying.

I realized as long as Doc was alive I could never relax; ten years of hitting and missing, the end was near. I could taste it just as strong as I could smell it, Doc's days was numbered.

I was sitting in a no parking zone when Felicia emerged from the Federal Court building, Chanel from head to toe, looking as sexy as she wants to be. I raised her from a puppy to a Pit; and there was nothing I couldn't ask of her that she wouldn't do; regardless if she had to put the pussy or the pistol on you.

"How did things go?" I asked and gradually pulled in traffic.

"Just as you said, the judge gave the government three weeks to put up or shut up."

"Good, good," I whispered. My mind was in overdrive, everything was falling in place. "Tomorrow you, Mike Loc, and Lil Buggs will be returning to Las Vegas. I need you to locate two stash house; one for our money, and the other for our weapons. Concentrate on a gated community with a 24 hour guard on duty; something preferably on a cul-de-sac, a short distance from Interstate 15, but more than 30 minutes from the strip. Be discreet."

It was a little over 80 degree with a slight breeze, the perfect weather for a poolside BBQ. I stepped out of my car and could hear the ever so cheerful sound of women laughing and water splashing. I followed the sound and paused at the gate enjoying the lovely sight of a pool filled with beautiful women playing volleyball. Monica climbed from the pool and greeted me with a warm, affectionate smile.

"Floyd I'm glad you came. Let me introduce you to my friends." She said and took me by the hand.

"Okay let's start with the youngest and cutest of the bunch, the little red head with the pretty freckles is Amy. The tall, brunette with the big bubbly eyes is Rebecca. And over here with the 44 double D's is our Latin princess Sophia. Now on the opposite side you have my baby sister Cathy, one of the sweetest girls you'll ever meet. And last but not least you have Elena, if you're ever looking for a house she is the one to see. Everyone this is Floyd."

"Hi Floyd," they shouted simultaneously. I acknowledged the group with a smile and a nod.

Hey Floyd we need another player, why don't you join us?" Amy said checking me out from head to toe.

"I would but I didn't bring a swimsuit."

"Who said you need a swimsuit to play volleyball." Sophia shouted, hoping I accepted her invitation.

"Don't pay them any attention." Monica said and took my hand and led me towards the patio where Alana was standing over the grill in the most revealing swimsuit I'd ever seen. Monica spoke so much about her I would have spotted her in a crowd of a hundred gorgeous women. Alana was everything Monica said she was, beautiful, sexy, and with a body that was designed to grace the cover of Sports Illustrated Swimsuit Edition. Her outfit complimented her attitude; Monica said she was a free spirit, it was easy to see.

"Alana this is Floyd; Floyd this is Alana."

"I'm glad to finally meet you Floyd, Monica talks so much about you I feel like I already know you." She said and extended her hand.

"Likewise," I said and accepted her hand. Like a stone cold flirt Alana slightly caressed my hand and stared in my eyes with the most seductive gaze I'd ever seen. Had I been a lesser man I would have been instantly captivated by her alluring charm, but I wasn't, I slid my hand back setting the stage for a game I knew we were destined to play. From the moment Monica mentioned her I knew she was a woman that strived off attention.

Monica said most men were like putty in her hands, and for some reason they just couldn't tell her no. Experience taught me the best way to handle a woman like Alana was to simply ignore her. Get inside her head and handle her like a simple chick. The longer you play her the harder she'll try to impress you.

"You got to watch her; she's one of the biggest flirts you'll ever meet." Monica said in a joking but serious manner.

"No I'm not," Alana said and paused, "okay maybe the second biggest flirt." Alana knew what she was about and made no secret of it. She enjoyed playing with men in an innocent sort of way, and I enjoyed playing with women in a serious sort of way.

Just as I was about to ask about their male companions four gentlemen arrived carrying a case of Budweiser and several large bags of ice.

"I hope the food is ready because I'm starving." A Spanish dude said and retrieved two beers. "Antonio," he said and handed me a beer.

"Floyd." I said and accepted the beer. After a formal introduction, all the men retired to the pool area to watch the women battle it out in a fierce three on three volleyball game. Monica rejoined her teammates while Alana remained at the grill.

It wasn't until the game was over and the women begin to pile from the pool I realized how truly unique each and every one of them were; each woman was a star among stars with each one shining just a tad brighter than the other. There was no mistaken Monica and Alana shined the brightest. Both women were extremely beautiful in their own right. Where Monica was lady like and blind to her beauty, Alana was just the opposite, a straight tease that was acutely aware of the power she possessed over men. This may have been Monica party but it was most definitely Alana's show. One thing I did notice that Monica didn't mention, not only were the men drawn to Alana, so were the women. I noticed the disappointment in Monica's eyes when I told her I had to leave, and I also noticed the excitement in her smile when I told her I'll be back in a few hours. There wasn't a day in the past two weeks we didn't talk, and there were many nights we talked until the sun came up. What started off as an innocent and sincere admiration had quickly developed into a quiet, intense affection, and everyone was starting to notice? I was feeling baby; yes indeed, how could I not. Outside of getting money, and laying my enemies down, there was nothing I enjoyed more than romancing a beautiful woman; and stimulating her every desire. I wanted her, and I sensed she wanted me; and there was no better time than the 4th of July to consummate our relationship

———————

It had been a while since I last spent some quality time with

Felicia, Akeelah, Yolanda, or any other woman I was romantically involved with. I couldn't deny I loved the chase more than the capture, and each woman provided something different and unique, but none had the complete package. I was taught never mix business with pleasure, but unlike most gangsters I played by my own rules, and unlike most gangsters every woman in my life played both sides of the ball. As long as I had their heart and mind, their pussy belonged to whomever I needed them to slide under. With the exception of Akeelah I was confident each and every one, especially Felicia would take a bullet for me. As admirable as it appeared, it simply wasn't enough; I needed more. Although it was too early to tell where Monica fit in the grand scheme of things, she appeared to have all the attributes I was looking for in a woman, a companion, a wife. So far so good but I needed to see more.

Monica had a lovely home, nicely decorated with a beautiful array of family portraits covering the walls. At first I was surprised she didn't have a TV in the living room, but after spending a few minute there I understood. The serenity and comfort I receive just sitting there was overpowering.

As I admired her beautiful furnishings it was clear she was a class act, and most definitely somebody worth pursuing. A woman like Monica only came around once in a lifetime if you were lucky, and lucky was my middle name. I took particular interest in a portrait of her and Alana. The artist had captured the true essence of each woman's beauty.

"How do I look?" She asked. I turned around and for the first time in my life was speechless. Standing before me, draped in a see through gown with red laced undergarments Monica was stunning.

"Do you like it?" She asked nervously.

"Like, no baby I love it." I said and opened my arms for her to come to me. She slid into my embrace and wrapped her arms around my neck pressing her entire body against mines. My lion responded immediately which seem to excite her even more. Our lips met, passionately at first, and then more aggressively as the seconds ticked away. I was trapped in the wonderful world of pleasure; everything I was feeling was new. Her touch, her smell, the taste of her lips were intoxicating, I couldn't get enough of her. Finally our lips parted, and without a word being spoken she took my hand and led me to the bedroom where we remained for the entire weekend.

Macking Gangsta
<u>Chapter 12</u>

Malcom Killebrew, better known as Mack was an old school hustler, a jack of all trades. Thirty-two years old and officially retired Mack had more game in his pinky finger than the average player had in his entire body. Mack was hands down the Godfather of Southeast with a mind as sharp as a razor and a mouthpiece that'll reduce a giant to a midget.

"Who got next?" I asked as I joined the crowd of spectators gathered at Skyline Recreation Center to watch Mack devour one victim after another in a friendly game of chess. Considered the best chess player in the city Mack kept an envelope on the table with a thousand dollars for anyone good enough to beat him.

"You got next." Mack said before anyone could answer. Shortly thereafter he turned towards his latest victim and whispered checkmate.

"Pretty Boy it's been a while since I last seen you, what's up with you Nephew?"

"You know me Mack, forever trying to stay ahead of the game."

"I hear you, what brings you around here?"

"Came to check you out, and steal a little knowledge at the same time."

"I figured that much." He cleared the crowd and waved towards the empty seat.

"What can you tell me about Vegas?"

"Vegas," he repeated and smile. "I've always known you had it in you. Some cats are born to pimp."

"Pimp," I laughed. "What gives you the impression I want to Pimp."

"Shit, why else would a playa go to Vegas? Outside of gambling, prostitution is the biggest game in the city. Sex or the illusion of sex is a billion dollar industry. Don't tell me you're going out there to gamble."

"No indeed. One thing I learned from you was the laws of gravity Big Bank take Little Bank ninety-nine out of a hundred times, and where I stand only a sucker would play them odds. I'm going out there to check out the scenery. I'm a lot of things Mack, a pimp I'm not."

"You speak on pimping and gangsters like you're speaking two different languages, in actuality they're closely related."

"How do you figure that?" I asked, curious to learn his thoughts on the matter.

"Let's talk about gangsters. I'm not talking about the average cat running around with his pants hanging lower than his ass. I'm talking about the real gangsters, the Mafia. The Mafia is about organized crime, racketeering. Do you know the three elements that define racketeering? Well let me tell you, it's gambling, narcotics, and prostitution, no matter how you turn it or twist it, it's all one in the same. When I hear a Nigga hating on the game I know he's not a gangster, he's a street Nigga that's pretending he's a gangster. Gangsters are about getting money; Pretty Boy I've been a gangster since I was fourteen, and I kept a crew of bitches on my team. Why do you think I ain't ever spent a day in jail, because my hoes did the heavy lifting, they kept me safe, and out of harm's way. If you plan on posting up in Vegas you've got to have some spotters, a few hoes to be your eyes, ears, and sometimes your muscles. A pretty bitch can open doors you and I simply can't get in, you feel my drift."

Mack and I sat there for the next three hours. He had the floor and I listened to every word he said like he was my favorite preacher giving his last sermon. One thing about good game it didn't need to be repeated nor explained. It didn't take much to make me realize the error of my ways. Suddenly I had a clear understanding of my next move. Just like I had a crew of young killers and guerillas, I was about to build a network of female villains; pretty as a motha fucka, too sexy to be denied, and will knock a motha fucka head off without a second thought.

There was something mystical and alluring about the city of Las Vegas. From the moment I stepped off the plane I instantly felt an overwhelming sense of excitement. Perhaps it was the bright lights, the lure of big money, or the prospect of matching wits with the coldest players that ever played the game, whatever it was I liked it. The night was still young and I had plenty of energy, and a whole list of places I wanted to see. After securing my rental car my first stop was a storage unit at the Greyhound station where I retrieved a 9mm equipped with a silencer and two boxes of shells that Felicia stored three days ago. Although I was over three hundred and fifty miles from the Hood, there was no telling who I might run into. My motto; if you stay ready you, need not to get ready.

At five hundred dollars a night the E-Suites at the Mirage was everything Mack said it was and more. I stood at the window overlooking the strip and enjoying the spectacular view. This was it, the life I always dreamt about. On all accounts, in the eyes of the streets I was a young gangster that made it. But to me this shit was penny ante. My dreams and desires extended far beyond this. I wanted the mansion, the horseshoe driveway with over a million dollars in exotic cars greeting my guest when they pulled up. The dynasty had to start somewhere; why not start with me.

I contacted Felicia and informed her I was in town and would catch up with her for breakfast. In the meantime there were a couple of spots I wanted to check out. One of them was the Crazy Horse 2 which was an exclusive gentlemen club that catered to top notch players and gangsters, and the one in which my last report indicated Cassie worked. Owned and operated by the Chicago Mob, bad attitudes and foolishness was checked at the door.

From the moment I step inside the Crazy Horse 2 I immediately recognized the attraction. The atmosphere couldn't have been more relaxing. 'Come and talk to me' by Jodeci was blasting from the high power speakers. Followed by Bobby Brown's "Humpin Around and En Vogue's Giving Him Something He Can feel." I cop a seat at the bar facing the stage and was memorized by a picture perfect white girl shaking her hips like she grew up on cornbread and grits. The Crazy Horse 2 was a European establishment, they played the latest R&B and Hip Hop hits; and by the looks of the crowd it was most certainly a winning combination. The majority of the men were suited and booted, or sporting smoking coats, jeans and loafers. I on the other hand came with the ball player look, a blue and white silk jump suit, with a pair of white K-Swiss and an eighty thousand dollar Rolex that'll wink at you from clear across the room.

I ordered a double shot of Hennessy and sat back and enjoyed the scenery. It was a lovely sight, a room full of beautiful women, just as elegant as they were sexy. Although the majority of them were Caucasian there was also a delicate mixture of Blacks, Asians, and Spanish women to enhance the appeal.

"May I sit down?" A beautiful Latina asked appearing from behind.

"You most certainly may." I said and smiled.

"I haven't seen you around here before, are you new in Vegas?"

"I just arrived today."

"Where are you from if you don't mind me asking?"

"Philly. What about you?"

"Seattle, and by the way I love your cologne. I don't remember the last time I smoked good weed. Do you have any for sell?"

"No baby I don't sell weed, but I'm pretty sure I brought enough to smoke with you. Forgive my manners may I buy you a drink?"

"Yes I'll take a glass of Chardonnay if you don't mind." She said and studied my reaction. Although I wasn't a frequent visitor of strip clubs I knew the dancers were taught to order the most expensive drink on the menu in an effort to give them an idea what type of money the patron were playing with. I turned towards the bartender and ordered her a glass of wine, and pulled out a nice size bankroll to pay for it. As hard as she tried to resist her eyes couldn't help but glance at the hand full of hundreds as I flipped through them and found a fifty.

"Thank you." She said when her drink arrived and quietly appeared to be pondering the best approach to play me out a few C-notes.

"My name is Melody." She said and ran her finger down my arm.

"Pretty Boy," I said and extended my hand, "how long have you been in Vegas?" I asked.

"I arrived six months ago."

"How do you like it?"

"I love it here. I make more money in a week than I made in a month back home."

"I can imagine; Las Vegas appears to be filled with possibilities. Did you come by yourself?"

"No, I came with my girlfriend Tiffany. That's her right there." She pointed towards a tall, slim, black girl giving a lap dance. Baby girl was good, a straight professional and perhaps one of the best dancers in here. I studied her moves and couldn't help but wonder could she fuck the same way she could dance. For the first time in my life I considered getting a lap dance; as pleasant of a thought I knew it would never happen. It was taboo for a gangster to put himself in a trick position. Paying for a lap dance was equivalent to paying for sex.

"Would you like to meet her?" Melody asked, after noticing the way I was staring at her friend.

"Maybe some other time, right now I've got my eyes on you." I replied studying her more carefully.

"Do you?" She said somewhat surprised. Although Melody was beautiful in her own right, she was no match for her friend, and it was obvious by her response she was acutely aware of it.

"Would you care for another drink?" I asked and decided to give her my full attention.

"Yes I'll take another drink, better yet let me buy you a drink."

"I'm starting to like you more and more by the second. Imagine how I'm ma feel in an hour. You might have me on a bended knee." I said bringing a smile to her face. Flattery was always the fastest way to a woman's heart. Back home Melody probably was considered drop dead gorgeous by the local standards. But in Las Vegas, surrounded by a sea of picture perfect bodies, and the most beautiful faces a woman could possess she was average at best.

Nevertheless I liked her style and I enjoyed her conversation. After her third glass of wine she was feeling kind of spunky. She couldn't stop laughing, nor could she keep her hands off me. She was feeling good; perhaps better than she had felt in quite some time. I looked in her eyes, she was ready.

"You ready to get out of here?"

"What do you have in mind?" She shot back and rubbed her hand up my lap.

"I got a room at the Mirage."

"Give me five minutes," she said and headed to the dressing room.

No sooner than Melody walked away a petite, beautiful young Asian girl sat down; Lil Mama was so pretty she looked like a baby doll. "My name is Paradise, may I join you?" She asked and placed her hand on my lap.

"I would love to chop it up with you but I'm about to leave, maybe next time." I said and removed her hand.

"You can't blame a girl from trying." She said and walked away when she seen Melody approaching. "I see you met Paradise?" Melody said when she returned dressed in a pair of shorts and flip flops.

"Yeah I met her; and it seem like she's strictly about her business."

"She is, don't let her innocence fool you. She might be young, but the girl got game."

It was amazing how a change in environment could bring about a change in appearance and attitude. Felicia adapted well to Las Vegas, I gave her the game and she ran with it. Dressed in a tennis outfit with a Gucci bag and a racket she looked like the daughter of a big time executive.

I rose from my seat as she entered the courtyard. I hadn't realized how much I missed her until I took her in my arms. This was my work, my creation, everything she knew I taught her. She trusted me with her heart, mind, body, and soul; she trusted me with her life.

"Daddy I miss you so much." She said and held me tight she didn't want to let go.

"I miss you too baby." I lifted her from her feet and swirled her body around. It was an emotional moment, and much to my surprise I felt a slight sensation inside my chest. Our relationship transcended the average gangster and girl union; we connected on every level, and had a genuine love for each other.

"Daddy I got a surprise for you." She said and glanced around the food court like she was searching for someone.

"What is it? Or shall I say who is it?"

Before she could answer I spotted Alexis approaching from behind her.

"Hey Pretty Boy," She said, looking as dazzling as ever. The party girl, punk rock look was gone; replaced by something far more sexy and sophisticated. I told Felicia to slide under her, I didn't tell her to give her a make-over. Felicia glanced at me looking for my approval. I gave her a smile and sat back to see where all this was going.

"What's up Lil Mama, this is the first time I've ever seen you without Mitch, where is he?"

"Fuck Mitch, I can't stand his trick ass." She shot back with venom so hot she didn't have to convince me she meant every word.

"I never seen that coming, I guess looks can be deceiving."

"He's changed Pretty Boy, he really has. Mitch is the biggest trick in the city. Every stint bitch in the city knows him. I feel embarrassed when I go out with him; and besides that these niggas be straight out playing his ass."

"How is that?" I asked, wanting to learn more.

"Three weeks ago we ran into this nigga name Tony, he owed us thirty thousand. Mitch refused to step to him so I did. The nigga slapped me right in front of Mitch, and told him he ain't paying him shit."

"I heard about that, and I also heard Mitch took care of his business." I said, knowing he did because I sent Lil Buggs to deal with Tony and let it be known Mitch was not to be fucked with.

"Fuck that Pretty Boy, if it wasn't for me he would have never called you. Mitch is a joke out here, no one respects him; I'm tired, I can't do it no more."

"Sounds like your mind is made up, if that's the case we'll leave that alone."

"It is, I swear on my life it is."

"Have you told him?"

"No not yet."

"Why not, what are you waiting on?"

"You," She said, capturing my full attention."

"Waiting on me," I smiled. "Is that right?"

"Yes, that's right Pretty Boy. I'm tired of fucking with weak niggas; I want to be with a gangsta. Someone I can feel safe with." She stared in my eyes, I seen all I needed to see. I could use a bitch like Alexis on my team; but at the same time Mitch's usefulness was far from over. From the moment she sat down my mind was in motion, Felicia had said Alexis wasn't happy and was thinking about bouncing on Mitch. Little did she know I needed her to stay where she was, as close to Mitch as possible. The last thing I needed was for Mitch to discover her defection.

"You know Alexis; I always looked at you like my sister." I lied as I finalize my next move.

"Well I don't want to be like your sister, I want to be one of your girls. I always told Felicia if I wasn't with Mitch I'll get with you. I'm no longer with Mitch and I want to be with you. I've felt like this since the first time I met you. I know Mitch is your boy, but with you or without you, Mitch and I are done. And to show you how serious I am I got something for you." Alexis opened her purse and slid a bulky manila envelope across the table. I glanced inside the envelope and handed it to Felicia.

"That's eighteen thousand." She said. "I wanted to give you twenty, but couldn't risk taking more than that. I hope that's enough."

"Mitch is making that much money he won't realize eighteen is missing. A motha fucka get me for ten dollars I want to know where it's at; everybody in the room got to get asshole naked." Felicia sat stone face while Alexis fell out laughing.

"You're crazy Pretty Boy." She continued to laugh.

"Felicia you better tell her, I'm not lying." I smiled and gave Felicia a wink.

"No girl he damn sure ain't; he's serious about his money, every dollar of it." She joined in on the laughter.

"Real talk baby girl. I like you, I like your style, but I am concern about your emotions, wearing your feeling on your sleeves; allowing someone, anyone to read your heart by looking in your eyes. I play this shit for real. I'm not a fifty-fifty, sixty-forty kind of gangsta, when I come to get it I want it all. First thing I want you to do is put this back, because that's my money anyway. "Next I need you to be the perfect bitch; instead of tripping off another bitch I want you to introduce him to a few more. My man got a million dollar operation and don't even know it. So far he's been fortunate, reckless to the point he haven't suffered any serious losses. I can straighten out his reputation, but in the meantime I will need you to keep a close eye on him. I want to know everything he's doing, everybody he's seeing; and at the same time I want you to slide under Dice and stay on top of him. Find out what's on his mind; is he really thinking about making a move on the club."

"He is he told me so."

"And why would he do that?"

"We messed around from time to time." She stated with the least bit of shame.

"Does Mitch know?"

"Yes, he was the one that asked me to, it was part of a deal; at least in the beginning anyway."

"You lost me right there."

"I only had to fuck Dice once to secure the loan; I liked it so I kept fucking him."

"Where do you stand right now?"

"We're cool; he's in LA right now. I'm supposed to hook up with him tomorrow night; do you want me to cut it off?"

"No, I need you to keep playing him, at least for another month. I'm about to make a power move on the club and I need to know how Dice reacts. Welcome to the family."

Melody was still asleep when I returned to the room. I stood over the bed and study the contour of her lovely figure. She was most definitely a beautiful woman, with a deep rich caramel complexion that complimented her long jet black hair. Although she was lacking in the ass department she made up for it with a set of Double D breast that the average woman would pay top dollars to have. Even the best surgeon in the country couldn't duplicate the feeling of real tits. I quickly disrobe and found my monster standing at attention. I never met a woman who didn't enjoy waking up to a nice hard dick.

I didn't know how Melody would respond after waking up from a night of weed, wine, and sex. I was pleased to discover she was just as willing now as she had been last night.

"How are you feeling baby?" I asked as I ran my fingers through her long black hair.

"I feel wonderful." She said and wrapped her body around mines.

"Do you?" I asked trying to feel her out.

"Yes I do, and I have you to thank." She said and ran her fingers across my chest. "I haven't been with a man in over a year. I almost forgot how nice it feels."

"I'm glad I was able to rehash fond memories. Where is your man in Seattle?"

"I don't have a man, I have a girlfriend." She said.

"That's interesting. If you don't mind me asking, are you talking about Tiffany?"

"Yes, that's my baby."

"You know you can call her if you like. She's probably been sitting up all night worrying where you been all night."

"No that's okay she doesn't call when she's gone all night. Now back to you, do you have a girl?"

"I got a few girls on my team."

"I didn't figure you for a pimp."

"That's because I'm not, I'm a gangster, but I do dip and dab in the game. Is that a problem?"

"That depends on you, and what you expect from me?"

"All I expect is for you to keep it one hundred. You get out what you put in. This game is about choice not force. The same way you walk in you could walk out."

"I had a man before, and he treated me like shit. When things slowed down in the club he tried to get me to sell my body, and that's something I'll never do."

"And that's something I'll never ask. I can't speak on your last man; all I can do is speak for me. I'm a family man, meaning my team is my family. I take care of my family like my family takes care of me. I'm not with no drama, and I don't play games. Just like there are certain qualities I look for in a woman, I'm sure there are certain expectations you expect from a man. Perhaps if you tell me what you're looking for, I can tell you if I can fill the bill."

"I'm looking for a man who will dick me down when I need it; hug and hold me when I want it. I work six days a week, and on Mondays I like to get my hair and nails done, and spend the day with my man. When you're with me, you're with me. What you do when you're not with me is your business. I'm not a needy chick, but sometimes I get lonely during the week and need some extra care. Can you handle that?"

"Baby I can handle anything under the sun, and I respect that. I love a woman that speaks her mind; put everything on the table and let a man know what the business is from the very beginning. I'm not going to sit here and hit you with some slick shit, it's not necessary, you play your position and I'm ma play mines, and I promise you we'll take this thing to the top."

Alana

Chapter 13

I quickly found myself spending the majority of my time in Vegas. As much as I hated to leave, I had obligations in San Diego I simply couldn't ignore; one being over three million dollars in investments, absent of my latest acquisition Floyd's Auto Finance & Lease. I started off with twelve cars, now I was pushing close to a hundred and quickly growing. I had Rick and Rob, twin brothers and two of the nicest hustlers in the city heading my sales department. The transition from crack dealers to car merchants came with the ease of walking and talking. Rob was the smoother of the two, but Rick wasn't far behind. Everything was a competition with them; especially car sales, which the company benefited the most. They set the standards for a healthy competitive environment. I had 14 permanent employees, all of which at one time in their lives were specialist in the street version of their department. The bigger the business the bigger their salary with the option they could buy back into the company; which plenty of them did. I learned a long time ago, people work ten times harder when they have an invested interest in the company.

The reception I received at the airport only reminded me how much I missed Monica, and how much she missed me. Upon seeing me she flew inside my arms and held me as tight as she possibly could. For a brief second I felt a small stab of guilt, while Monica was home missing me every minute of every day, I was in Las Vegas having the time of my life.

"Come on baby let's get out of here." I said and released her.

"What about your luggage?" She asked, appearing somewhat confused. Little did she know I had none, but right now was not the time to explain? I wasn't here to stay; as a matter of fact my return flight was scheduled to leave in less than 24 hours. I ushered Monica out the nearest exit and pretended like I didn't hear her. My plans were to take her to dinner, followed by a night of dancing and love making. Tomorrow she would have the option of relocating to Las Vegas, or staying here in San Diego. With less than a week until her graduation my timing couldn't have been more perfect. I didn't have the slightest clue of how she would respond to my proposal, but one thing I did know, with her or without her my days in San Diego were numbered.

One thing I admired about Monica she knew when to talk and when to listen, and she also knew when to ask questions, and when to leave it alone. From the moment we left the airport I sensed something was bothering her. I knew she was concerned by my lack of luggage, but to what extent? Had I known her only fear was me leaving her I would have eased her concerns immediately. Being that I wasn't certain how she would respond towards moving to Las Vegas I waited for the best opportune time to bring it up, which usually occurred during pillow talk, immediately after a session of raw intense sex when a woman was most susceptible to any suggestion.

"What's wrong baby?" I asked as she laid her head on my chest.

"Nothing," she whispered, "I just miss you so much."

"I miss you too baby, but I can tell something is bothering you. What's on your mind, let's talk about it?"

"I feel like things are changing between us. I feel like you don't love me the same."

"I don't love you the same, I love you more, more and more every day."

"Do you?" She asked and propped her arms on my chest and stared in my eyes.

"Baby I don't know how you can possibly question my love; have I done something I'm not aware of?"

"Floyd you were gone almost a month, what were you doing out there that was so important it kept you away from me?"

"Baby I was laying the foundation for our new life, in a new city." I said and studied her reaction.

"We're moving to Las Vegas?" She asked excitedly.

"Yes we are." I answered as if it was a planned surprise. Monica never ceased to amaze me, especially on important matters. Every time I questioned her response I was far from the mark. From the moment I met her it had been about me, my dreams and aspirations. Whatever I was down for, baby had my back.

The following week Monica and Alana drove to Vegas to take a look at four properties. She selected a five bedroom home in Spanish Trail, a gated community west of the strip. While Monica was busy overseeing the move, I was on a serious mission, learning everything I could learn about the city, and the hustlers that called Vegas home. I had so many females on my line I couldn't remember all their names. Every night, five days a week you could find me posted up in one of Las Vegas exclusive gentlemen clubs shooting my shot at the sexiest bitch in the club. Black, white, brown or yellow it didn't matter to me I had something to talk about. I was confident in my Mack game, and I knew if a bitch sat down long enough I had her.

There simply weren't enough hours in the day for me to do all the things I wanted to do. Macking and playing was about trickery, painting pictures, and selling dreams. The average woman shaking her ass on a pole, or letting a stranger lay between her legs wasn't the type of women you took home to meet your mother. Macking and love was like oil and water, it didn't mix. Pimping 101, you can't turn a hoe into a housewife, let a hoe be a hoe.

There was no better job than to get paid doing something that you'll do for free. I guess you could call it the battle of the sexes. Mack taught me 95 percent of all men were tricks and the other five percent represented the three horsemen. The player, the preacher, and the politician, all of whom got paid from conversation. The cold part about it, the player was the most honest and admirable amongst the three.

I arrived at Monica and wasn't surprise to discover Alana's Infinity parked in the driveway. It was a little after midnight, the odds of Monica being sleep, and Alana being awake was highly likely. No sooner than I stepped inside Alana emerged from her bedroom in her panties with a cut off T-shirt.

"Where is Monica?" I asked as my eyes travelled the length of her body resting on the dark bush between her legs.

"She's sleep." She said and smiled.

"I see you're not going to stop?"

"Stop what," she asked innocently.

"You know what I'm talking about?"

"I'm afraid I don't. Are you talking about the way I dress, do I make you uncomfortable?"

"No you don't. Unlike the majority of the men you've been dealing with I've never been a sucker for a pretty face."

"So you think I am pretty?"

"You're cool, but you're not my type."

"I think you're lying, I can see the way you look at me, and to be honest I think it's flattering."

"I don't know what you think you see, but it's obvious you read me wrong. Word of advice; don't confuse suspicion with lust, because they're not remotely related. I give it to you, you're a nice looking woman, but I have seen better, and besides you're a little too thin for my taste. You have a good night."

I left Alana standing there looking more confused than ever. She had finally met her match, a gentleman on the surface, but a stone cold player in disguise. Unbeknownst to her I've been in the presence of some of the slickest bitches on the planet. Unlike her it wasn't fun and games, it was real life shit where a bitch was trying to trim you out your bankroll or your life. It was evident by the distraught look on her face Alana wasn't a woman accustomed to rejection. If that's all it took to rattle her cage then flipping her was going to be a lot easier than I thought.

Little did Alana know she had my blood pumping in a way it took every bit of restraint to maintain my composure. She had awakened a breast I couldn't simply put back to sleep. I thought about taking a cold shower, but quickly decided against it when I entered the bedroom and found Monica sound asleep with the covers halfway down her beautiful nude body with one leg outstretching the other. I pulled the covers down exposing her entire body. Her ass was nice and plump I wanted to bite it. I quickly undressed and slid between her legs. On the verge of losing control I subdued myself by running a trail of warm wet kisses from her shoulder up her neck and along the side of her face, while running my manhood between the folds of her love nest until she moaned and open her eyes. Before she could say a word I was inside her. She accepted me with cries and moans of pleasure which seemed to grow louder the deeper I pushed inside her. Tonight wasn't about making love; it was about hood passion, the type of passion that only a gangster could put down properly.

You know you took care of business when you wake up and find your girl singing in the shower. I stepped in the shower and was greeted by the loveliest creature on this planet. I reached for the soap and Monica took it from my hand. I've never had a woman bathe me and pay so much attention to every detail of my body; especially my scars which made her frown and kiss each one twice as if it would magically disappear. She knew her man was a gangster, and it was my past that made me the man I was today. Even so her heart bled for the shit I been through, and for those reasons and so many more my love for her seemed to grow stronger by day.

Alana was sitting at the dining room table nibbling on a grapefruit when we emerged from the bedroom. For the first time since I met her she wasn't in her happy go lucky spirit. It was obvious something was bothering her. Perhaps it was the way I shot her down, or maybe it was the fact that she was standing outside our bedroom door listening while I was putting down one of the best performances of my life. Whatever it was, it was only the beginning of a journey that was destined to have her at my beck and call.

"What's wrong Alana?" Monica asked and ran her hand down the side of Alana's face.

"I don't know; I didn't sleep well." I think I'm ma call in sick today." She said and kissed Monica's hand. The love and concern was visible. They were close, closer than any two women I'd ever known. As I sat there and quietly observed this intimate exchange I couldn't help but wonder was there more to this picture than I was seeing.

Monica was by far the most important woman in my life, and an intricate part of my future plans. The Game of Gangsters wasn't designed to play forever; and at some point, when my bankroll was right, I needed an exit plan. Although she contributed the least financially, what she brought to the table couldn't be measured in monetary gains. She was the complete package, extremely beautiful, highly intelligent, and blessed with a heart of gold, what more could I ask for?

I was making so many moves between Las Vegas and San Diego it was hard to pin me down. The more time I spent at Monica's the more

Alana seemed to hang around. My presence there didn't alter her behavior, she still ran around the house in her panties and bra like it was the most natural thing on the planet. I couldn't deny baby girl had a sex appeal that'll drive the average man crazy; but there was nothing average about me. I tried to understand Monica's take on the situation but she gave no indication she felt threatened or bothered by Alana flirtatious ways. It was a strange situation, the first I ever encountered.

As hard as Alana portrayed to be the Boss Bitch in full control of her life I could see right through her. Like most women she had her doubts and insecurities that she just couldn't seem to conquer. Regardless of how much I ignored her, Alana continued to run around the house in the skimpiest outfits she could find. I had to give it to her, she refused to give up. My first act of kindness came the morning Monica was flying back to San Diego to celebrate her Mother's birthday.

Alana emerged from her room and was surprised not only to find I had made breakfast, but I made breakfast for her also. The same amount of care and affection I served Monica, I served her. My actions were so surprising both women looked and smiled.

"I was thinking when you get back the three of us can go out and celebrate."

"That'll be wonderful." Monica said and reached out and squeezed my hand. It was a heartwarming moment, one that appeared to be the beginning of a long awaited healing period between the two most important people in her life. Even Alana seemed elated by my change of attitude. Little did she know I was about to flip the game on her. Alana was far too sexy and far too beautiful not to play with. Although I had a number of beautiful women on my team, none of them could hold a candle to Alana. She already had the talent; she just didn't have the skills. Under my guidance I was more than confident in my ability to flip her from a mere dick tease to one of the sharpest bitches the city ever witnessed.

I took Monica to the airport and returned and discovered Alana had washed the dishes and cleaned up the place rather nicely. This was a major feat coming from a woman who swore she'd never washed a dish in her entire life.

"What a surprise." I said and inspected her handiwork.

"Well that's the least I could do, after all you made breakfast, and I must say it was quite delicious."

"Thank you, I'm glad you liked it. You know it's almost nine, shouldn't you be heading to work?"

"I should, but I'm not. If you haven't notice I go to work when I want, and get off when I want, and still get paid the same."

"How you manage to pull that off?" I asked even though I already knew the answer.

"I guess you could say the boss has a thing for me." She said with a flirtatious smile."

"Your boss and every other man you come in contact with."

"That's not entirely true," she said and paused. "I know one man that doesn't find me attractive at all."

"And who might that be?" I asked.

"I'm speaking of you." She said and stared at me a moment. "You know today is the first time you've ever showed me any kindness. Up until now I thought you disliked me, and I didn't have a clue why?"

"I'm sorry I made you feel that way, but believe me when I say that is truly not the case. Baby you are one of the most beautiful woman I've ever laid eyes on, but I'm ma keep it real with you, it's not your beauty that I question, it your intentions. You play so many games I feel like I must keep you at a distance. I feel like you're waiting for me to approach you the wrong way so you can run back and tell Monica."

"Pretty Boy I swear I'll never repeat anything you tell me. Yes I love Monica with all my heart, but I don't tell her everything that's going on in my life."

"Let me ask you something? You have so many male admirers what is it about me that gets you so roused up?"

"I'm not used to people ignoring me; looking at me like I don't exist; it bothers me. You made me cry several times, and I just couldn't seem to understand why. Pretty Boy you're so different than any man I've ever met; I love the way you carry yourself, and I love the way you treat my friend. I'm jealous; I wish I had someone like you. You're a real man, tough and aggressive, but also respectful and kind."

"So that's the type you like, the Gentleman and the Gangster type?"

"What girl doesn't?"

"I guess we both been checking each other out. Check it out baby, go get dressed and let's take a ride."

While Alana was getting dressed I made a few phone calls that I was more than certain would leave a lasting impression on her. Unlike most women in my life Alana posed a rare and very unique challenge. Her entire life she had been the recipient of other's affections, praises, and gifts; even Monica's. I couldn't recall one time where she was the giver of anything. From day one it was about her, and she didn't lead anyone to believe otherwise. She carried herself like royalty with entitlements; she met her match now.

Check Game
<u>Chapter 14</u>

I never been a club type gangsta, it wasn't my style, and besides it was a security risk for a man that had as many enemies as I did; but I couldn't deny I fell in love with Club Nuevo the moment I stepped inside the huge Industrial Warehouse. The structure alone provided five star security; and didn't give the slightest hint of what lied inside. Three bars, two stages, and a VIP lounge that accommodated the biggest players, pimps, hustlers, and gangsters. The floor area was equally impressive with six glass enclosed platforms that showcased the most energetic dancers I ever seen; they kept the party goers hyped. As enticing as it appeared I had no personal interest in Club Nuevo, it was simply a legitimate acquisition I could pass on to Lil Bull, the ultimate people person. Before doing so I had to eliminate all previous threats.

It didn't take long to realize there was no Club Nuevo without Mitch; he was the one they came to see. Mitch was gifted with a set of musical skills that took instrumental to a whole new level. Never in my life have I ever seen a Cat so cold with a turntable and a microphone. Mere words could not adequately describe the frenzy before my very eyes. I turned from the window at the sound of the intercom.

"Yes." I answered.

"Boss, Dice have arrived."

"Send him up." I smiled and proceeded towards the elevator. Under different circumstances it would have been a sheer joy to see Dice; there was a time when we were Comrades in Arms, two young soldiers climbing the ranks of CCO, and catching each other back with our lives. Unfortunately our previous alliance didn't transcend to the free world; we were living in a time where Crips were killing Crips, and Bloods were killing Bloods; anything or anyone outsides one's hood was fair game.

"Supreme greetings Cuz, glad you could make it." I said and embraced the homie.

"Back at you Cuz." he shot back and smiled. Besides his weight not much had changed with his appearance or mannerism. He still walked with the confidence of a gangster on top of his game. It had been years since we last touched base, and in the crime game a lot could change in that amount of time. Only Dice knew his intentions, and for the sake of fond memories I hoped they were good.

"Please have a seat Cuz." I said and waved towards a set of red oak leather chairs.

"Daddy would you care for something to drink?" Sassy appeared from the back with a smile that was designed to place the hardest gangsters at ease.

"Yes I'll take a cup of coffee, how about you Dice?" I asked and didn't take any joy in the gloomy expression on his face. If he had any doubts concerning my status here they were laid to rest. This was my spot.

"I'll take the same." Dice said and quickly regained his composure. "I like it, I like it. I'm impressed."

"Appreciate it Cuz. We use to talk about this life, now we're living it. This is only the beginning; before it's all said and done we're going to rewrite the game."

"You know it, so what brings you to the surface?"

"You," I said and paused. "You were pressing my boy so hard, I had to step forward before it got too far out of hand."

"You did the right thing because I was about to put a full court press on Mitch. Mitch told you about our arrangement."

"That's over with, effective immediately." I said abruptly.

"Cuz I need that plug, at least for a few more months."

"I wish I could help you but I can't. Had I known Mitch was laundering drug money through my club I would have knocked his head off?"

"Cuz this is kind of sudden, I wasn't expecting this, nor am I prepared for it."

"Cuz you know life is about adjustments; sometimes we got to stop on a dime and switch gears. As much as I'd like to accommodate you the risk far outweighs the gain."

"Sorry to hear that." He said after a brief silence. Dice had his poker's face on and I found it hard to read him. Based on past experience I had a strong sense this was far from over. After another hour of futile conversation Dice rose to his feet, promised to get together later and made a quiet exit. No sooner than he left Tye Stick, Mike Loc, and Lil Buggs emerged from the next room where they were monitoring the entire exchange.

"Cuz I don't trust that Nigga, I think we should kill him and get it over with." Mike Loc said which surprised no one. With Cuz murder was the answer to all problems, regardless how big or small the situation was.

"I got to agree with Mike Loc." Tye Stick added. "I was studying Cuz the entire time, never took my eyes off him. Cuz was too motha fucking cool, and obviously not the type of Nigga that take no for an answer. I think we should put some security on Mitch, and it won't be a bad idea for you to tighten up yours until we get a wrap on things." I nodded my agreement and turned towards Lil Buggs.

"Cuz you know me, I don't give a fuck one way or the other. You give the word I'll hit Cuz tonight." Lil Buggs shot back looking for the green light.

"In event we got to hit Cuz we got to dress it up, and it most definitely can't happen in Vegas. The last thing we need is a war, or be the focus of a police investigation. This is not Cali; the undercovers out here is rolling in Benzes, sporting Rolexes, and coming like street players. Every move we make got to be on point, and under their radar. If everything goes as planned by this time next year we'll have the city on lock. Mark my word."

My resume was written in stone, but unlike most bosses I still approached the Crime Game with a student perspective; always in search of knowledge, a better and smarter way of conducting my business. Suspicious by nature my trust was limited to a chosen few, men I have known my entire life, all of whom I've experienced a life and death situation, and broke bread with in the penitentiary as well as in the free world. It was too late in the game to meet and trust new people, as far as membership the books were closed. Although I had love for the women in my life, past experience taught me to keep them at a distance; close enough to touch them, but far enough where they couldn't cross me.

The more time Alexis spent around Felicia the more she begins to mimic her style, which was a good thing. I studied her poise as they approached and nodded my approval. Felicia did a good job grooming her, far better than I expected. It was amazing how a woman had the ability to transform her entire look with a different color, a different cut. Prior to hanging with Felicia, Alexis was already pretty but plain, a Valley Girl with purple hair and more piercings than a punk rocker. Half Cuban and half white her now jet black hair complimented her Latina heritage and supported her deep rich tan. Based on the amount of time she was spending with Dice it was obvious I wasn't the only one that appreciated her new look.

Although Felicia assured me Alexis was all about me I simply couldn't ignore the possibility she may be a plant, a double agent, pretending to do my bidding, while at the same time representing Dice best interests.

"Good evening ladies." I said as I rose to my feet and greeted both with a hug and a kiss on the cheek. "You ladies are looking absolutely lovely."

"Thank you Daddy." They said simultaneously.

"Would you care for a cocktail?" I asked and wave for a waiter.

"Yes, I'll take a Rum and Coke." Alexis said, and quickly changed her mind after Felicia shot her a glance. "I'm sorry." She said and giggled when she realized alcohol and business was strictly frowned upon. "I'll take a Raspberry Frost Soda."

"I'll take the same." Felicia repeated.

After placing their orders I directed my attention at Alexis. "Now what's so urgent it couldn't wait another day?"

"It's Dice Daddy, lately he's been asking a lot of questions about you. This morning he called and said he really needed me to find out where you lived, or where you hang out ASAP. He suggested if all else failed the next time I see you or hear you're in the city to call him immediately regardless what time it was."

"That's interesting; so far what have you told him." I asked studying her every move searching for deception."

"Pretty much nothing, I told him exactly what Felicia told me to tell him, I've only met you on a few occasion, and each time was during a meeting with Mitch, in which I wasn't allowed to sit in. I also told him I hear you were in Vegas a few days ago, met with Mitch, and whatever you told him scared the shit out of him."

"You did well, always keep it short and simple, never give a mother fucker anything to feed off, keeps em guessing." I said and turned towards Felicia, who was waiting impatiently for her moment.

"Alexis could you give us a private moment, there is something I need to discuss with Pretty Boy."

"Oh sure, I'll be waiting by the bar. Bye Pretty Boy, it was nice seeing you again."

"You too Baby girl, once we resolve this matter with Dice we'll be spending a lot more time together."

"I'll like that." She said with a smile that left much to be desired. I turned back towards Felicia expecting to find a frown, a hint of jealousy, but instead she was also smiling, which I found odd but refreshing; perhaps this was the beginning of a new era, one where she played her position and accepted all aspects of a Gangster's life.

"You did a good job with her, I'm impressed."

"Thank you Daddy, it wasn't hard, she's eager to please."

"Do you think she's ready?"

"As ready as she'll ever be."

"Alright set it up, I want Dice dead before the end of the month. Take your time, I need to put some distance between his death and my last meeting with him. In the event we got to get rid of two bodies instead of one I want Mike Loc and Kenwood to run point. Once you arrange everything get at me before you make a move. Understood?"

"Yes Daddy, understood."

"The grand re-opening of Club Nuevo was the hottest spot in the city; although under new management, Mitch was still the man and his followers came out in droves to support him. With the exception of a few new faces and tighter security not much had changed. It was shortly after 2am when Dice's Crew arrived ten deep, and unlike the past they all had no problem paying the $20.00 cover charge. The homies were fourteen deep scattered around the club like party goers, armed to the tee and ready to move at the first sign of aggression. No one and I meant no one was permitted to enter the club without going through the metal detector, which left no one but the homies with their hardware. Dice was a smart man and I was sure he realized, just as I, a physical altercation inside the club would be detrimental and serves no one's best interest. In the meantime it was a cat and mouse game, the only difference; Dice thought he was the cat, when in actuality he was the mouse.

I was back in San Diego, but San Diego no longer felt like home. Las Vegas presented many comforts but when it came to security nothing could compare to the safety one felt in his own Hood. If a gangster got knocked in his own Hood he was meant to perish. Regardless of the threat, big or small I took it serious. I came too far and been through too much to allow a nigga to clip my wings. From the very beginning I was in it to win it, I love the game, it was pretty as a mother fucker when you was winning but ugly as a bitch when it flipped on you; yet instead I wouldn't trade it for nothing in the world. This wasn't a game where the toughest and hardest prevail; this was a game where the smoothest and the sharpest came out on top; but getting on top wasn't the problem, staying on top was.

The reception I received at the airport only reminded me of how much I missed Monica, and how much she missed me. Upon seeing me Monica flew inside my arms and held me as tight as she possibly could. For a brief moment I felt a small stab of guilt, while Monica was home missing me I was in Las Vegas having the time of my life.

"Come on baby let's get out of here." I said and released her.

"What about your luggage?" She asked, appearing somewhat confused. Little did she know I had none, but right now was not the time to explain? I wasn't here to stay; as a matter of fact my return flight was schedule to leave in less than 24 hours. I ushered Monica out the nearest exit and pretended like I didn't hear her. My plans were to take her to dinner, followed by a night of dancing and love making. Tomorrow she would have the option of relocating to Las Vegas, or staying here in San

Diego. With less than a week until her graduation my timing couldn't have been more perfect. I didn't have the slightest clue of how she would respond to my proposal.

One thing I admired about Monica she knew when to talk and when to listen, and she also knew when to ask questions, and when to leave it alone. From the moment we left the airport I sensed something was bothering her. I knew she was concerned by my lack but to what extent? Had I known her only fear was me leaving her I would have eased her concerns immediately. Being that I wasn't certain how she would respond towards moving to Las Vegas, I waited for the best opportune time to bring it up, which usually occurred during pillow talk immediately after a session of raw intense sex when a woman was most susceptible to any suggestion.

"What's wrong baby?" I asked as she laid her head on my chest.

"Nothing," she whispered, "I just miss you so much."

"I miss you too baby, but I can tell something is bothering you. What's on your mind, let's talk about it?"

"I feel like things are changing between us. I feel like you don't love me the same."

"I don't love you the same, I love you more, more and more every day."

"Do you?" She asked and propped her arms on my chest and stared in my eyes.

"Baby I don't know how you can possibly question my love; have I done something I'm not aware of?"

"Floyd you were gone almost a month, what were you doing out there that was so important it kept you away from me?"

"Baby I was expanding the business, laying the foundation for our second home. How does that sound?" I said and studied her reaction.

"Floyd I'll follow you to the moon if you ask me to."

"I know you would, and I wouldn't go unless you came. Monica never ceased to amaze me, especially on important matters. Every time I questioned her response I was far from the mark. From the moment I met her it had been about me, my dreams and aspirations. Whatever I was down for, baby had my back.

The following week I sent Monica and Alana to Vegas to lease a spacious five bedroom two story home in Spanish Trail, a gated community west of the strip. While Monica was busy overseeing the move, I was tracking Dice every move, learning everything I could learn about his business and the people he recently had beef with. It was imperative his murder didn't come back on us. One thing about the streets the underworld didn't need twelve mother fuckers to find you guilty, usually the last person you had words with got credit for your murder if he did it or not. I receive no joy plotting the murder of a Crip legend, but it was Dice, not I who threw the first stone.

It was a 4-hour drive from San Diego to Las Vegas, and no one knew I was in the city except Alana; sexually I just couldn't get enough of her. Alana made a gangster want to stay in bed all day. Like a wild, untamed cat Alana met me stroke for stroke, moaning, biting, and scratching as I pushed deep inside her. Alana was dick hungry, love fucking more than a fat kid love cake. With each encounter, the guilt associated with cheating with her best friend gradually faded. Monica didn't have a clue what was going on between Alana and I; nor did she know I was back in Las Vegas. As much as I enjoyed Alana's company the thought of leaving Monica never crossed my mind.

Drenched in sweat, I rolled over and stared at the ceiling. I was drained, completely spent, and satisfied by all means. Had I not known Alana was a virgin a month ago I would have never believed it. Baby's skills in the bedroom were unbelievable; and unlike any lover I ever had, her pleasure came from my fulfillment; and her unselfishness encouraged me to explore her body in ways I never imagined. Every inch of her body had a different flavor, but her pussy had a taste sweeter than a southern peach. It was time to put her to the test, and it was how she responded to this test that would determine where we went from here.

Alana was standing at the window watching the Pirate Show from the 60th floor of the Treasure Island Hotel and Casino. One thing I loved about her was the excitement she displayed when experiencing something new. When happy she had the most beautiful personality a woman could ever possess. It didn't matter where we were, or what we were doing she seemed to lighten the moment. I enjoyed her company.

102.

"Come here baby," I said and open my arms. Without hesitation, Alana slid inside my embrace and wrapped herself around mines until every part of our bodies was touching.

"Are you ready for round seven?" She asked and took my manhood inside her hand.

"It's more like round ten if you count last night."

"I can make love to you all day and night. I love the way you feel inside me; it's like we were meant for each other."

"I know exactly what you mean, and I feel the same. But you know there is a whole lot more that comes with me. It's obvious we have a strong connection, but the million dollar question is are you ready, ready for a man like me?"

"Yes I'm ready; I've been ready, can't you tell?" She said and giggled.

"I most certainly can, but sometimes looks can be deceiving, I rather hear it than see it that way I know for sure."

"What would you like to hear, how happy I am, how much I love you, how I'll do anything in the world for you? Daddy, I love you so much, I get goosebumps when you touch me."

"Is that how you really feel?" I asked.

"Yes that's how I feel; you're everything I've ever wanted in a man. You're tough when you need to be, but you're so much more when you don't have to be. When I'm with you, there is no other place on earth I'd rather be, and when I'm not with you, all I do is think about you. I live for the moment to see you; to hear your voice, to make love to you. Yes, I love you, do you love me?" She asked like she was doubtful of my answer.

"Baby I fell in love with you the first day I met you." I lied.

"Did you really?" She said and stared inside my eyes.

"Yes my love, look at you, how could I not?"

"Daddy I know you're a player, and I know Monica and I aren't the only women in your life. I would love to have you all by myself, but I know that's not going to happen; at least not right now. I enjoy missing you because I know the next time I see you I'm ma feel a hundred times more excited. You do something to me, and I love it. Daddy the only thing I ask of you is to never lie to me. If I'm with you for a month, a year or the rest of my life let it be because that's what I choose, not because of a lie. Do you understand what I'm trying to say?"

"Absolutely, and spoken like a woman that knows exactly what she wants. Let me pull your coat, only soft-hearted and weak men lie, gangsters don't. From me to you, if you keep it real with me, I will keep it real with you."

"Pretty Boy I love you, I'll do anything for you."

"Will you?" I asked as I studied her more closely.

"Yes, anything, do you doubt me?"

"Of course not, I can see it in your eyes; I can hear it in your voice. Staying on the subject there is something I can use your help with."

"I'm listening?" She sat up and suddenly became serious with a look that said tell me more.

"I need you to slide under Councilman Byron Williams; it shouldn't be hard being that you already know him."

"Yes I do, I know Byron quite well, and not just as Monica's ex-boyfriend; Byron and I have a history of our own."

"Okay you've sparked my curiosity, what are you not saying?"

"Well you know I moonlight as a Dominatrix?"

"Yes, you mentioned it." I said, paying close attention to her every word.

"What you don't know is that Byron is one of my best customers.

"You're shitting me!" I shouted and bust out laughing. "I had a feeling there was something strange about dude. Who else knows about this?"

"Only you and I hope you don't mention it to anyone. I like our arrangement, and I must add it pays very well."

"As long as he cooperates I see no reason in exposing his freaky ass. When was the last time you saw him?"

"Last week. I usually see him every other week, depending on his schedule."

Once Alana started talking I couldn't get her to stop. She had an interesting tale to tell, one that involved some of the kinkiest shit I've ever heard. Byron was a freaky mother fucker and just one of many high-profile tricks in Alana's little black book which she willingly gave up. At the moment I was only interested in Byron, and concocting a strategy that would force him under my control. It wasn't hard convincing him to run for District Attorney, being that his platform and new found fame was built on Crime Prevention. In the eyes of society, he single handily eliminated violent crimes and drug sales in Southeast San Diego. I had big plans for Byron; my vision far exceeded his ambitions. If elected D.A in less than 5 years my aims would be on the governorship.

Playing with Fire
<u>Chapter 15</u>

I was waiting in the hangar admiring the fleet of private jets when a dark sedan entered. Normally today would have been a day of celebration; it wasn't every day a gangsta walked out a federal court a free man with no attachments, but as the circumstances would have it the party would have to wait. A smile appeared on my face when Lil Bull exits the vehicle looking like a big ass Grizzly Bear. I studied my man as he approached, it didn't take more than a glimpse to recognize the seriousness behind a humble smile. It was an eye-opening experience, one that made a man appreciate all aspects of life. In many ways, I was happy my man tripped over his own feet. There were certain lessons a man could only learn in the midst of severe adversity.

"Welcome home Cuz." I said and gave my dog a huge embrace.

"Thank you, Cuz." Lil Bull whispered in my ear and tightened his embrace. Mere words could not express his appreciation. He knew what it took to get him out, and even now it was hard for him to fathom I was able to pull it off. This was my brother, giving up on him was equivalent to giving up on me.

"It goes without saying baby boy. There was no way in the world I was about to let you die in there."

"Cuz you went far beyond the call of duty, best friends and brothers. I was hit, and I saw no way around it. Cuz I was 5 seconds away from copping out to thirty-years. I accepted it, but there was something in your voice when you said don't do it."

"Cuz the Feds want 85 percent, twenty-four years and ten months off of thirty. They lost their rabbit ass mind, that's a life sentence. A gangster would be old and gray before he came home, I'd rather be dead."

"I feel you on that. Check game Cuz we're running a little late, you've got a connecting flight at Oakland International; in the briefcase, you'll find your license, passport, and a hundred thousand dollars in U.S. currency, and fifty thousand in traveler checks. Your family is waiting on you; give me a call when you get there."

"Will do; and once again thank you Cuz."

"You know how we do it, have a safe trip Cuz." I wanted to spend more time with my Road-Dog, but I realized the quicker he shook the city, the less likely the Feds would be able to put an eye on him. An hour after Lil Bull departed for Australia I boarded another jet heading back to Las Vegas.

Monica and Alana were waiting at the airport for my arrival. I couldn't tell who were happier to see me; Monica or Alana. For a brief moment I wondered how complete life would be to live, love, and grow old with these two beautiful women. It was most definitely something worth thinking about. Individually they were unique and special in their own right; but together they were everything I ever desired in a companion and more. How lucky could a man get?

Alana stood impatiently and waited for Monica to release me before she gave me a hug that seemed inappropriate and suggestive. Reluctantly I hug her back and search Monica's eyes to see if she was feeling uneasy? She was. Being the lady she was, she kept her concerns to herself and said nothing about the exchange. It was at that moment I realized I had a live wire on my hands. Alana wasn't the type of woman that kept her feelings in check, to ask her to do so would in a sense be asking her to change the very essence that made her who she is. True enough I wanted her in my life, but at what expense?

Later that evening when we were all alone in the comfort of our bedroom Monica laid her head on my chest and ran her fingertip across my stomach which was a clear indication something was bothering her.

"What's wrong love?" I asked as I rub my fingers through her hair.

"Nothing," she softly murmured.

"Come on baby I can sense something is bothering you. I don't know why you feel you can't talk to me. I hate to see you like this; what's bothering you?"

"It's Alana." She said and paused. "I think she's got a thing for you."

"What makes you think that?"

"The entire time you were gone all she talked about was you. Then the scene at the airport, she was so happy to see you; if I didn't know better, I would think you two were having an affair. I've never seen Alana act that way. I'm telling you, Floyd, I think she's got a thing for you."

"I can't see it, but I must say it's kind of flattering. To be honest, I got the impression she didn't like me."

"Baby you got to know Alana to understand her. I've never met anyone she didn't like. Alana has always been overly protective of me, especially when it comes to men."

"Is that all it is?" I asked, switching the subject and setting the stage for a conversation I'd longed to have with her.

"What do you mean?" She asked and propped her arms on my chest.

"I get the feeling at some point you and Alana were more than friends. Am I right?"

"Yes there was a time when we were more than friends; does that bother you?"

"No, should it?"

"I don't know; some men find it repugnant."

"Well I'm not some men, and I find it kind of arousing; to be honest watching two women getting it on has always been a fantasy of mine."

"Is that what you like; to see two women making love, or do you want to participate?" She said with a boldness that seemed to shatter her innocence.

"It all depends." I said and studied her more closely.

"Depends on what?"

"I guess it all depends on you and your ability to watch me with another woman without getting upset. Can you handle that?"

"Yes I can handle it; don't laugh but the thought of you with another woman is making my pussy wet." She smiled and ran her hand between her legs and slowly rubbed her pussy. Damn my dick was hard. "Do you have someone in mine?" She asked and continued to play with herself.

"The question is do you have someone in mine?"

"To be honest, all my friends would jump at the opportunity to have sex with you. My girls and I talk about everything, and everything includes you. They know how happy I am, and they also know you're the reason behind my happiness. Most of my friends do not think of sex in a traditional sense, with them it's more of a physical stimulant than an emotional attachment. Just as I trust you, I trust them. I know a moment of lust would never lead to something more serious; nor would it complicate what we share. As a matter of speaking, I think it would strengthen our bond. Am I making any sense?"

"You're making plenty of sense."

"Which one shall it be?" She asked unable to control her excitement.

"How about Alana since you think she got a thing for me?" I asked as subtle as possible.

"Alana." She said and paused. "Baby anyone but Alana. Alana is like my sister. I know you probably won't believe this, but Alana is a virgin. Even if she was willing; and she probably would be, I couldn't handle the thought of my future husband busting my best friend's cherry, it would complicate things. You do understand?"

"Yes, baby I understand; all your friends are gorgeous, anyone you select will be fine. Surprise me."

"I will, and I promise it'll be a night you'll never forget."

"Well if that's the case I promise you tonight will be a night you'll never forget."

I sat at the bar and admired the subtleness in which Cassie handled her business. Today was her 21st birthday; the stage was covered with so much money they had to sweep it up. She was escorted off the stage like royalty and continues to collect money from everyone she passed. Just as quick as it touched her fingers, she handed it to her collector that was stuffing it in a bag. I rose from my seat the moment we made eye contact. "Happy birthday Lil Mama;" I said and placed a small package inside the palm of her hand. She gripped it gently, smiled and kept walking without knowing what was inside it. Melody told me she loved ecstasy and would fly to San Francisco at least once a month to score. If that was the case her flying days were over because we had the best Ecstasy in the country; baby blue Doves by way of Amsterdam.

It was unbelievable how crowded the stage area was when Cassie hit the stage. Cassie was the best in the business when it came to simulating a masturbation scene. Baby girl put on a show, one that was guaranteed to have every dick in the house with a hard-on. Club Paradise was the perfect venue for her. A Gentlemen Club where most patrons were suited and booted, top-notch executives, where million dollar deals were sealed, and the club tabs ran into the thousands on the company's dollar.

Cassie had an infectious personality, with a smile that was alluring, and a laugh that seemed to draw you closer. There was absolutely far more to her than meets the eye; on the surface, she gave the impression she was as gentle as a kitty cat, but in actuality, she was a Tiger and had more game than any bitch in the club. I couldn't help but admire and respect the way she conducted her business. After observing her for nearly a month, and unable to find a casual opening to whisper in her ear I laid in the cut like a professional poker player waiting on a pat hand.

I was still sitting at the bar when she emerged from the dressing room garbed in a sexy fire red Cat Woman's outfit. After shooing off a few patrons, she smiled like she was happy to discover I was still here. From the moment she learned Melody had a weed and ecstasy connection, Cassie been on her back begging her for an introduction. We had the best weed and ecstasy on the west coast and were very particular who we did business with.

"I'm so happy you're still here." She smiled, exposing her true youthful features; she was a pretty little bitch. "I wanted to thank you." She continues. "That was most certainly the perfect gift."

"I'm glad you like it."

"Like it, I love it, and here I thought my 21st birthday was going to be the wackiest of all. Twenty tabs of ecstasy, and the fattest and prettiest bud I have ever seen, you saved the day Mr. Blue Dove?"

"You like them huh?"

"They're the absolute best; they're just so hard to find."

"Well from this moment on that's one less worry you have."

"Thank you, but why?"

"Because I really enjoy your performances, and it would only take a phone call to make it happen."

"You really haven't witnessed one of my actual shows; there is only so much we can do on stage would you like a private show?"

"No, I'm good Lil Mama."

"I'm sorry that didn't come out right. I wasn't trying to solicit you, you've already been quite generous. I was merely suggesting it's more comfortable and private in the VIP, and the dances are on the house, my way of saying thank you."

"That's not necessary; the smile on your face is thanks enough."

"I insist." She said and took my hand. Unable to deny her, I rose to my feet and followed her to the VIP section.

Lil Mama was aggressive, which I liked. I trailed slowly behind her, fixated by the way her hips swung and her cheeks danced to a beat of their own. Young, petite and all so sexy Cassie had a body you could play with in any position. A smile played across my face as I envisioned easing 9 inches of hard dick inside her. Cassie was a young woman, living her life, getting her money, and mastering the art of trickery. She was a fantasy, a dream that most of her clients paid big money to chase. I sat back and sipped on a glass of champagne, the first glass passed with few words, a subtle observation followed by a sense of curiosity. I was feeling Lil Mama, she was a hustler, and she brought something different to the table. It was a shame the odds of her surviving what I had instore was slim to none. "Happy birthday Sunshine," I said and held up my glass.

"Thanks to you it will be; are you going to celebrate with me?" She asked and produced two tabs of ecstasy.

"I most certainly am," I whispered and locked eyes with her. The longer I stared, the more enticing she became. At 5 feet three, petite with a figure that had my lion pressed harder than penitentiary steel and begging for release.

"Hey, hey, that's my song!" Cassie shouted excitedly as Keith Sweat "You may be young but you're ready" blared from the stereo. I sat back like Don Corleone and enjoyed the show. She was on me, sliding her body across mines ever so gently. We did everything but penetrate. If I didn't know better, I would have sworn it was my birthday.

I looked at her stomach and wondered what the hell she was talking about. It didn't dawn on me until I observed a small pug in her lower abdomen.

"Is that what I think it is?" I asked in a state of bewilderment.

"Yes, it's exactly what you think it is. Floyd you're going to be a father; I'm six weeks pregnant, are you happy?" Alana shouted with a smile that lit up the room.

I received her news with mixed emotions; on one hand, it was the best news I could have ever imagined, and on the other hand, I couldn't help but acknowledge the implications; and what it would do to Monica once she found out.

"What's wrong Daddy, you don't look happy?" She said.

"Baby I'm ecstatic. As happy as I am I can't help but wonder how this will affect Monica; she's going to be devastated."

"No, she's not, she going to be overjoyed; trust me, baby, I know."

"What makes you so certain?" I asked in a desperate attempt to ease my concerns.

"Monica can't have kids, and that's one thing she wants more than anything in this world. The best gift we could give her is a child we can all share and raise together; don't you agree?"

"I really hope it's that easy because I can't stand the thought of hurting her. I love her to death; it would crush me to see her cry."

"Do you love me?" She asked and searched my eyes.

"Yes, I love you," I said and smiled. "How could I not, you're my baby mama. I feel like the luckiest man on the planet."

"I'm so happy you're happy. Don't worry Daddy I promise everything will work out."

Alana's words of encouragement seemed to bring a small measure of comfort. As much as I loved and cared about Monica, another chance at fatherhood trumped everything. What I wanted most was to have my cake and eat it too; but in the event that wasn't possible, Monica could ride out.

The sky was the limit; I was on point, enjoying all the benefits associated with being on top of my game. Unlike San Diego where I had the mark of the beast, Las Vegas provided me the opportunity to come all the way new, with a fresh legitimate profile; one that I hoped would convince the court to grant me equal custody of my only child; something I knew Nicole would fight tooth and nail to prevent. There really wasn't any sense in trying to reason with her, and being my son's mother busting her head open was out of the question. I had to play it fair, do it like it's supposed to be done, by society's rules, let them white folks tell her she's got to share.

Lil Bull
Chapter 16

On the surface I was a successful businessman; beneath I was a Crime Boss, a stone cold gangster; a Ruler over niggas and bitches. Every female I had on my team played their position, it was understood, point seen money gone, it was about me. Akeelah was my ace in the hole, sharper than a double-edged sword, with a business sense, none could match. Businesswise she was on point, capable of handling anything I slid her way. I liked baby, twenty years my elder she could be difficult at times, but for the most part, she kept me grounded, and on top of my game.

I pulled up at Akeelah's mountainside home overlooking the beach. It was a beautiful sight with a nice ocean breeze. Oscar and Bruno, her two Rottweilers, rushed the front door before I could get one foot in the house. I knelt down to show them some love. Oscar was my favorite, the smaller of the two, but more aggressive. I was still playing with them when Akeelah stepped into the entrance dressed in one of my button-down shirts with the sleeves rolled up. Still kneeling I had an up-close and personal visual of her beautiful shaved pussy.

"Why you didn't tell me you were coming home." She smiled and slightly parted her legs.

"You know I love to surprise you." By the time I stood up my stick was rock hard.

"Look at you; you're about to bust the seams out your pants. Come here and let me take care of that."

She didn't have to tell me twice; Akeelah's body was soft and smelling good. She pushed me up against the wall and slides her tongue inside my mouth. Our tongues met savagely, danced around each other creating a heat you could have lit a fire off of it. I slid my hand between her legs and manipulated her clit until she moaned from pleasure. She was wet, leaving my fingers wet and sticky. I cuffed her cheeks and lifted her in the air. I didn't have to tell her, Akeelah held on tight and took every inch I slid inside her. She worked that pussy, squeezing and pulling, sliding up and down. She tried to position herself, but I wouldn't allow it, I pushed so deep inside her she lost her breath. "You want this dick baby," I whispered in her ear as I pounded that pussy. "Yes I want it, give it to me Daddy."

Whatever plans she had this morning were canceled. They say absence makes the heart grow fonder, and I must concur. It felt refreshing to lay there and hold this gorgeous woman inside my arms. The serenity I felt at Akeelah was just what I needed after a month in Las Vegas. Only Felicia knew where I was, and for the exception of a severe emergency, this is where I planned on chilling for next week. Outside of a few scheduled meetings, my calendar was free.

Truth be told rest and relaxing wasn't the only thing on my mind when I popped up at Akeelah's; like all things in my life it was never an occasion when my personal moves didn't solve a business purpose. Not only was Dice and Akeelah comrades, they were from the same set. I've been in the midst long enough to know never question one's loyalty to one's set, or put em in the position to betray it. It was time for Dice to go, and I could find no better alibi than Akeelah to verify I had nothing to do with it. The big homies had been transferred to New Folsom, B-Facility, and they were trying to reestablish old alliance. Tabari was aware how deep Akeelah was under me, that's what he originally hoped for; what he didn't wish for was my independence, I saw no benefit reestablishing ties with CCO, I was doing my own thing and there could only be one Boss. Still his wife, I didn't involve myself in their business. Akeelah managed their relationship outside my presence which was only fitting. We both held past connections and loyalties to people other than each other, and I was cool with that.

After a short nap, and a nice lunch Akeelah and I headed to the beach. A short trip down the mountainside put us right at the edge of the Pacific. Like two kids still in their teens, once we hit the sand the race was on. A former college track star Akeelah got a quick jump, but I was right on top of her. Damn, she was fast, but not fast enough. I overtook her and went airborne into the semi-cold water. Lake Mead couldn't compare to the Pacific Ocean. Tomorrow we'll invite a few friends, pull out the jet-skies and ride from sun up to sun down; build a beach fire and chill.

I had five residences I could chill at; Akeelah was the least of my possessions but the one spot where I felt most comfortable. It was all about that square life, absent of gangsters and guns. The ultimate goal was to be legitimate with a bankroll that'll survive four generations.

I nodded my approval as I look over the documents giving Lil Bull sole ownership of Club Nuevo. I wanted Cuz to have a business, one that I knew he would enjoy running; and one that would be able to justify our way of living. We were flipping money so quick going legit we gladly gave Uncle Sam what he had coming. Money looked more beautiful clean than it did dirty. It was my job to develop new and inventive ways to clean it and keep it growing. The government didn't give a fuck where it came from as long as you paid taxes on it.

From the moment Alexis introduced Felicia as her friend Dice made it no credit how much he would love to enjoy them both at the same time. Like most gangsters with a large bankroll Dice showed his affections with expensive gifts, and travels to getaways that were meant to be impressive and show how he was coming. At 5 11, 138 pounds Felicia had a body that was designed to arouse. Everything about her was sensuous; long pretty legs with an ass that jiggled so perfectly with every step she took. Lust was known to weaken a gangster to his knees and convince him to succumb to shit a sharp mind would have prevented. I lost count, how many niggas lost their lives chasing a piece of pussy, Dice would be no different.

Victorville was two hours from LA and two hours from Vegas, the perfect meeting place, and also where Dice had three homes; all designed for a particular purpose. His ranch-styled, red oak home was the perfect place to entertain, a place Alexis had frequented many times. Dice was known to divulge in illicit drugs; he enjoyed popping pills, especially Ecstasy and Sand Bars; not to mention the GHB he took regularly, right before sex. Known to take it a little too far on occasions Dice kept one of his bodyguards on deck when he was partying. Felicia only agreed to advances after he promised her it would be the three of them at the house. After taking the first of several X, they stripped and got in the Jacuzzi. Dice was so mesmerized by their nudeness; he didn't notice that neither women swallowed their pill. Dice couldn't keep hands off Felicia, he wanted her so bad he didn't notice Alexis leave and return with a bottle of Tequila and 3 shot glasses, nor did he notice the two powerful caps of GHB at the bottle of his glass when Alexis bust the cork and poured him a shot.

"What are we toasting to?" Alexis said and filled everybody's glass to the top.

"Let's toast to a night he'll never forget!" Felicia shouted, jumped up, allowing her tits to bounce in Dice's face. Dice's tongue shot out like a dog lapping water trying to catch one of her nipples in his mouth. Felicia grabbed him by the neck, shoved her nipple in his mouth and quickly released him when she noticed he was about to spill his drink. "Here's to us!" Only Dice turned his shot glass upside down while Felicia and Alexis allowed most of the alcohol to seep out the side of their mouth. Dice already had one cap of GHB in his system, two more caps was more than enough to lay him out. It didn't take long for his speech to slur and his motor skills to give way, paralyzing him from the neck down. After desperately fighting to keep his head erected, he finally gave in allowing his head to rest peacefully on his chest. Without delay, Felicia and Alexis pulled him by the legs allowing his head to slip beneath the water. Without struggle or any type of resistance, death would come quick and peaceful, as if one died in their sleep. While Dice lied motionless underwater Felicia and Alexis went about the tedious task of eliminating all traces of their presence. A half of bottle of GHB with Dice's prints was left on the side of the Jacuzzi; that combined with ecstasy and cocaine in his system was enough to render an accidental drowning.

I was over-looking the Transfer of Ownership papers to Club Nuevo when Akeelah hung up the phone and turned towards me. The papers appeared to be in order, she did a spectacular job. Not only was she my girl, my friend, my lover, she was also my financial manager, privy to the majority of my financial holdings. Normally she had a thousand questions concerning every transaction, but this one she had none. I thought that was odd, something I would later reflect on.

"Come here, baby," I said and patted my lap. Akeelah smiled and rose to her feet. My last day was always a somber moment, the sadness in the back of her eyes was always visible; she couldn't hide it even she tried. This time felt different.

"What's wrong love?" I asked and rubbed my hand down the length of her leg. As always her skin was soft as cotton and smooth as silk. Our bodies felt good together like they were meant to be touching each other.

"They found Dice dead this morning. From what I gathered he drowned in his Jacuzzi. He must have been high; I've always warned him about those drugs. Dice liked to party with white people, ain't no telling what he was messing with. I remember one time he asked my son did he know where he could get some ecstasy. People don't know what the hell they're putting in them pills and they're popping them like candy. I've known Dice his entire life, at one time him and my son was very close. But when he came home he was different, damn near worse than Zuberi; the only difference was he was selling his poison out of town instead of in the hood. I wanted him gone, but I knew Tabari would never sanction a hit on his cousin. Nevertheless, I'm still a little sad he's dead, Tabari will be crushed." She turned and looked in my eyes. "I don't want you to go." She whispered and wrapped her arms around my neck. "Can't you stay another day?"

"I wish I could baby but I can't, I've got too much lined-up. Why don't you come back to Vegas with me?"

"No, no, I like it like this. When you come here, I have you all to myself; I just wish you stayed longer."

The last day was also a time of reflection, consolidating my thoughts, and preparing to jump back in the Lion's den. Akeelah was at peace, smiling in her sleep, and enjoying her afternoon nap. Everything was perfect except the last day, as strong as Akeelah was she always got musky when it was time for me to leave. After gathering my belongings, I kissed her on the forehead and made my move. I jumped in the Benz and dialed Alana as I was pulling out the driveway.

Prior to leaving I told Alana I was about to go under and I'll be unreachable for the next seven days. That didn't stop her from blowing up my phone every day hoping I'd answer. She most definitely had some ways that I wanted to erase. By the volume of missed calls, she'll give the impression it was a dire emergency when in fact she just wanted to hear my voice. She picked up on the first ring like she knew it was me. "I see I've got to change my number, to stop you from blowing up my pager."

"You better not." She said and started to giggle.

"Alright, you've got my undivided attention, what's so important it couldn't wait until I got home?"

"Daddy I just missed you so much. It feels like you were gone forever, and besides, I'm starting to show. I don't know how much longer I can avoid Monica; I think we should tell her, the longer we wait, the harder it will be on her."

"Sound like you've given this a great deal of thought, what do you suggest?"

"If it's alright with you, I think I should be the one to tell her. I think it will go a lot better if we had a girl on girl talk, without you being there."

"That might not be such a bad idea," I said, taking the coward's way out. No one knew Monica better than Alana, and if she thought this was the best approach I was inclined to believe her; and besides I wasn't sure my presence would help matters. How could I explain impregnating her best friend? I committed the ultimate act of betrayal; an act so vile I couldn't get mad if Monica decided to wash her hands with the both of us.

Unlike a hood chick, I figured Monica would cry until her eyes were incapable of producing tears; at which time she would emerge from a state of depression and latch out at anyone close to her. In a desperate attempt to understand how the two people she cared the most about could betray her she would search for blame; herself first, Alana second, and third the man of the hour. Fearful of losing both she would find herself in a position to choose, and that's where I'd lose.

My first thought told me to let her go, cut my losses and concentrate on building a new life with Alana. As beautiful and sexy as Alana was I simply didn't love her. Monica was my baby, the one person in the world I looked forward to seeing, and being with. If there was any way I could salvage our relationship, I would. It wasn't my style to give up without a fight; especially on someone worth fighting for.

The Sun was just going down when I pulled up outside baggage claim and didn't have long to wait before Lil Bull emerged through the sliding glass doors. Although, I had love for my entire crew Lil Bull was my dog, my best friend, the one I would bet my life on. If you knew me, you knew him.

"Welcome home Cuz?" I smiled and relieved him of his suitcase.

"Glad to be home, never realized I could miss the city so much."

"There's not a place on earth you can compare to home," I said and stopped at a black on black, drop-top 600 SL Benz.

"I figured you were getting money, but not like this. This bad boy is clean; I know I'm good to roll it in from time to time."

"You can roll in it all day, every day if you want. Welcome home Cuz, that's you." I said and threw him the keys.

"Damn Cuz." He said and smiled. "Thank you Cuz."

"Glad you like it, let's rolls. Are you hungry?"

"Yes indeed, as a matter of fact I've got a taste for some Baby Back Ribs."

"Sound good to me, and I know just the place, but we got to make a quick stop first." It didn't dawn on me that I forgot the papers to the club until I was already at the airport. Akeelah's was a little bit over an hour away, and Huntington Beach had a few spots that served some of the best ribs in Southern California.

"North or South, point me in the right direction and I'll get us there." Lil Bull said excitedly like he couldn't wait to hit the highway and see what the Benz could do.

"Huntington Beach." I said and turned up the stereo bumping Dr. Dre featuring Snoop Dogg- "Nuthin but a 'G' Thang.)

"Who's that sitting in the car?" Akeelah asked, breaking her neck to see who it was.

"Where did I leave the papers to the club?" I asked and brush right past her without answering.

"I don't know, check upstairs." She said, still trying to see who was sitting in the car.

I rushed up the stairs and immediately noticed something different about the bedroom. It appeared as though Akeelah had done some decorating after I left. I paused at a huge portrait of her and a small boy who I assumed to be her son Clifford who got killed a few years back. Being that she never mentioned him, I never asked about him. For some strange reason he looked awfully familiar; unable to put my finger on it, I moved to the next picture which was a solo picture of the boy a few years older. I removed the picture from its hook and studied it more closely. Clifford was a handsome young man with his mother's features. Had he been alive I'm pretty sure with a mother like Akeelah he would have been on top of his game. I opened the nightstand drawer and discover the manila envelope I came for, and several more pictures of Clifford accompanied with his obituary. Confusion quickly turned to concern the moment I realized I was staring at Chagina, the CCO homie Lil Bull killed when CCO came at him. I dropped the pictures and rushed back downstairs. No sooner than I hit the bottom of the stairs the unmistaken sound of a 357 Magnum rang out, hitting me with an overwhelming surge of fear. I reached for my 9mm and emerge from the house to discover Lil Bull's lifeless body slumped over the stirring wheel with the top of his head blown off.

"I'm sorry Daddy, I had to, he killed my baby." She murmured as a stream of tears rolled down face. I slowly removed the gun from her hands and took her inside my arms.

"It's okay love," I whispered in her ear and ran my fingers down the center of her back, gently caressing her until her body stopped trembling. I was shook, dazed beyond disbelief, my Dog was gone, slaughtered before my very eyes and it was my fault.

"Baby we got to get rid of his body," Akeelah whispered, bringing me back to reality. I cuffed her face and lifted her head. 'Damn, I thought as I looked in her eyes and quickly pushed her away. "Floyd," she pleaded with a confused expression on her face. She knew it was over, there was nothing on God's green earth, that could save her from this wrath I was about to unleash upon her. My first four shots ripped into her chest with such velocity, the impact lifted her from her feet and threw her lifeless ten feet backward. I felt nothing as I stood above her and unloaded the remainder of my clip into her face leaving her beyond recognition. The distress I felt wasn't satisfied by her death; the loss of Lil Bull would haunt me until my last day on this earth.

The reality of my present situation hit me like a ton of bricks; suddenly complete silence turned into a loud noise like I was snapping back from a dead state. The police were on their way, and perhaps already on Mountain Side Road. I had to get out of here, and my best bet was on foot.

My mind was racing a thousand thoughts per minutes, nothing made sense. As much as I needed to concentrate on my escape I couldn't erase the images of Lil Bull's slumped over the steering wheel. I was no stranger to death, there was no hood in San Diego that had suffered more losses than the East Side Neighborhood Rollin 40's Crip Gang, but this was different, the loss of Lil Bull was like the loss of a blood brother, a best friend, and homie all rolled into one. Trapped in an area I wasn't familiar with sorrow would have to wait another day; right now I was fighting against the clock, and time wasn't on my side. Under the cover of darkness, I rushed down the mountainside and could hear distant sirens growing louder by the second. My first order of business was to put some distance between me and the crime scene. The last thing I needed was to get jammed up in Huntington Beach, where blacks were a small minority and could be spotted blocks away. I arrived at the bottom of the mountainside and quickly removed the empty clip from my gun and replaced it with a new one. Even though I had a fresh murder on my gun the thought of dishing it was not an option. A gangster without a gun was like a pilot without a plane. I knew me, and as long as I had my gun the odds of escape multiplied a thousand times over. I felt for anyone, police included, that stood in the way of freedom. I was confident once they identified the victims I would be on top of their list of Persons of Interest.

Not only was my fingerprints inside the Benz, my fingerprints; and other items identifying me could be found inside Akeelah's home. It was just a matter of time before the authorities came knocking.

I couldn't believe the game flipped on me like this, one moment I was on top of my game, chasing my paper, and making it happen? Now I was trapped in a situation I couldn't say for certain how it would turn out. A sick laughter escaped my lips; I don't know why I felt so surprised, even the hardest sometimes came up short in the game of Killers and Guerrillas. I briefly analyzed my present situation and concluded it was essential I avoided arrest as long as possible. I needed a sound proof alibi, one that would sustain the closest scrutiny. True enough they could tie me to Lil Bull and Akeelah, and place me inside the Benz and inside Akeelah's home, but they couldn't place me at the crime scene at the time of the murders; nor would they be able to able establish a motive. I had a lot of loose ends to tie; in the meantime and in between time I had to disappear, go underground until I was ready to face the music; and there was only one person I could trust, one person that had the resources that could make it happen, and that was the big homie Malcom Killebrew.

You can run, but you can't hide
<u>Chapter 17</u>

Malcom sent Karen, his number one draft pick and wife of 15 years to come get me. He understood from the call, it was a Life or Death situation, one that he had only one person he could trust with my safety and get me where I need to get to figure this shit out. Karen pulled up at the restroom on the side of AM/PM; knocked on the door four times signaling the coast was clear. Karen was sitting in an Astro Van with the engine roaring when I jumped in the back and lay across the seats. I closed my eyes, not concerned where we were headed, I trusted Mack with my life.

Time seemed to stand still as I replayed the day's events inside my mind. This was one of those times a gangster prayed it was a bad dream, but knowing when he opened his eyes the nightmare would just begin. This was a moment where you questioned everything and everybody, even yourself. There was no do over in the Crime Game, regardless of what hand you were dealt you had to play it. Looking back all the signs were visible, Akeelah always showed a strange interest in Lil Bull, knowing what I know now I wondered did CCO ever issue the hit on Lil Bull. The

Big Homies knew how close Lil Bull and I were. Even if they would have, I'm sure they would have never included his wife and kid, and they would have never chosen me to execute it. I was now certain it was all Akeelah's doing and had I looked into it I could have prevented everything.

I opened my eyes the moment the van stopped, and she killed the engine. "We're here," Karen said and opened the door. I stepped out the van, stretched my arms and legs, and took a deep breath of the fresh mountain air. Mack was sitting in front of the fireplace sipping on Cognac and staring into the fire.

"Floyd would you care for something to eat or drink?" Karen asked.

"Yes, I'll take a double shot of Hennessy on the rocks." I said and took a seat across from Mack.

"Thank you," I whispered and meant every word of it. I was indebted to Mack; I couldn't remember how many times, in the course of my life he came to my aid.

"You're welcome nephew, anything you need just say the word. I should have the papers you requested by tomorrow afternoon. I suggest you get some rest, clear your head, it's always better to look at things with a fresh mind. Karen will show where everything is, and I'll touch base with you at breakfast. Good night nephew."

"Good night Mack."

The double shot of Hennessey took the edge off, but the pressure was still intense. Unable to clear my head or shake the day's events I sat there staring into the fire desperately trying to formulate a strategy that would bring me some measure of comfort. There was nothing more painful than losing a loved one; it was a hurt that seemed to weigh you down and permit you from gathering the strength you so desperately needed to battle. I was built for battle, in the courtroom, or on the block, the venue didn't matter. In order to move forward, I had to figure out where I went wrong and put in place safeguards to make sure it never happens again. Two of the closest people to me were gone in a flash.

Violent murders usually preceded a form of arguing, fussing, or fighting; in the murder of Lil Bull, there was no verbal exchange. My dude left the earth never knowing why?

Sleep was calling but I couldn't answer, my mind was overloaded with questions I didn't have the answers to. The first 48 hours were crucial in a murder investigation, the period in which most murder charges were decided, and it was most definitely a time where I needed to be my sharpest. I could still feel the weight of the world pressing down on my shoulders when I ran off the first of three thousand push-ups, which turned out to be just what I needed. I showered and hit the bed; sleep came quick.

I was well rested by the time morning came. The aroma of dark, rich fresh brewed coffee made me rise to my feet. I found Mack in the kitchen about to put it down.

"The smell of freshly brewed coffee has been known to wake a man from his sleep."

"You know it; top of the morning Unc." I said and grabbed a cup.

"Good morning Nephew; did you get some rest?"

"Most certainly; it's hard not to in a peaceful environment."

"Grab a seat and let me make you one of my famous Spanish omelet.

"You don't have to tell me twice, feel like I haven't eaten in a year."

"Good, because they're pretty big; there is some freshly squeezed orange juice, milk, and more beverages in the frig help yourself; my home is your home. Sorry about Lil Bull, I know how tight you were."

"Yeah, my dude caught a raw deal; with things the way they are I won't be able to attend his funeral."

"I'll have Karen send a nice arrangement in your regards. I will be gone most of the day if you need anything call, Karen, she's just a few minutes away."

"I need a clean line; I got a few calls I must make."

"I'll let Karen know, you should have one within the hour."

Absent of big city noise Big Bear provided the perfect environment to collect one's thoughts. Based on past knowledge and experience, once all the facts came to light, I was certain I would rise as their number one Person of Interest. It was my job to make sure it went no farther than that. Preparation was the key to developing a winning strategy; my mind was collecting and analyzing data; breaking down that fatal day, re-examining every moment, arranging and studying each frame, I needed to know what they knew; and they could only know what the crime scene told them. I was the only living witness, the only person privy to every detail leading up to the murders. The crime had already been committed, what lied ahead was the investigation, trying to establish a timeline, followed by a battle of legal minds. I couldn't change the events that transpired prior to this moment; moving forward it was essential I stayed 3-4 steps ahead of the game, they catch up they win.

I felt a lot better knowing I had Mack on my team; my man was as sharp as they came, a Master of the game; and his wife Karen only added to his brilliance. Mack was about his business and a man that paid attention to detail. No sooner than he left Karen arrived with a satellite phone that couldn't be traced. I not only needed eyes and ears in places I could no longer visit, but I also had to create a defense, an answer for every question, and an alibi that'll stand up under the closest scrutiny. Monica was my go-to girl, the woman I trusted the most; the church girl, the schoolgirl, the working girl, the perfect person to catch my back.

"Hello Love." I said the moment I heard her voice.

"Floyd where are you? I thought you said you were coming home last night."

"I was, but something came up. Check it out baby I got a situation on my hands, and I need to see you."

"Where are you?"

"I am ducked off; I'm ma call you in a few days with instructions where to meet me. In the meantime, I need you to start getting everything together, and I need you to bring me a hundred thousand all in hundred dollar bills.

"Why so much, what's wrong?"

"I'll explain when I see you. If anyone asks have you seen or heard from me, you tell them no. You understand?"

"Yes Daddy." Immediately after hanging up I felt a chill run down my spine. My senses were on high alert, looking at everything. After replaying my brief conversation with Monica, I was certain something was wrong. Monica sounded strange, and for the first time since we been together she hung up the phone without saying "I love you." The last thing I needed was another situation to analyze. Unable to determine the cause of my latest fears I decided it may be a figment of my imagination, and pushed it to the side.

Tender Roast Beef, with mash-potatoes and gravy, sweet corn, and string beans completed the meal. Malcom put in 14 hours, came back and made a four-course meal. The table was set for three, me him, and Karen. This was a family moment, a moment of friends, and acknowledging the tight bond we share. Business was never discussed at the dinner table; dinner time was reserved for pleasant conversation, jokes, and moments that make you smile and laugh. It was a time to relax, push reality to the side and lavish in the moment.

Mack and I retired to the study while Karen tidied up; he wasted no time bringing me up to date on the latest developments. I wasn't surprised when Mack informed me Law Enforcement obtained a video from LAX showing me picking up Lil Bull at 7:15 pm. Huntington Beach Police Dispatcher received their first call of shots fired in the Terry Pine Mountain's area. At 9:10 pm. At 9:25 pm Patrol Officers Gonzales and Warren arrived at the crime scene and discovered the deceased bodies of Kenneth Payne and Akeelah Donovan. From 7:15 to 9:10 was five minutes short of two hours, damn sure not a lot of time to work with. This presented a problem, one I had to figure out. Mack also informed me based on the evidence they couldn't determine if I was a victim or the perpetrator. Homicide detectives had more questions than answers. I liked my chances, had I not; I would have been on the first thing smoking out the country

I owed Mack big time, he was just one of a chosen few I called a friend. Unlike most, my definition of a friend differs from others. A friend to me was one I could trust with my money, my life, and my wife. If they fell short in just one category, they became an associate. Five days later I was on my way with a new identity. In order to put my defense in effect, I had people to see and places to go, and I still had an Empire to run. I had qualified people in every position, operating independently and also in concert. Detectives were knocking on new doors every day and were coming up short. People couldn't tell them something they didn't know.

I was making all the right moves, touching base with all the right people. I was ready no matter how they plan on coming. I had the entire weekend reserved for Monica, she was my number one draft pick, the one I relied on the most. I glanced at the wall clock and realized she wasn't scheduled to arrive for another three hours. I was posted up at the Embassy Suites where we had three out of four managers on the payroll. Although convenient and comfortable I only intended on staying two no more than three days; then on to the next spot. I was traveling light, rolling a new Ford Taurus and sliding in and out of traffic without a blink. In times of uncertainty business always came before pleasure, and that's the main reason Alana was the last person I touched base with. Baby girl was turning out to be a needy chick, one whom I didn't have the time she requires. Her affection was cute in the beginning, but smothering at times. I had to break her of the bullshit and lace her boots my way. I've been molding females since middle school, getting her right would only require a gift for gab.

"Good morning sexy." I tried to remove the stress from my voice.

"Baby I'm sorry, you got every right to be mad at me." She blurted. "I didn't think she would react so hateful. She said she didn't ever want to see me again."

"Hold up, what are you talking about?"

"I'm talking about Monica; I've never seen her so upset. I was so wrong; I thought she would be happy, we could have all lived as one and raise our baby together." I listen to every word and couldn't tell if Alana was naïve to believe that Monica was going to be cool with her man impregnating her best friend, or was this part of a clever scheme to rid Monica from my life. Either or it was a situation where she couldn't lose.

Had Alana not mentioned it I would have never known Monica knew about us. She played it off smooth; as a matter of fact, she played it too smooth; but why? Monica wasn't the type of woman that held anything in. She wore her emotions on her sleeves; children and animal lover, she had the biggest heart of any woman I ever knew. What was she up to?

I lost count how many times the phone rang, just as I was about to hang up, Monica answered. "Baby what are you doing at home; you should have left over two hours ago?"

"Floyd I'm not coming; I don't ever want to see you again." Her voice trembled as she tried to maintain her composer.

"Baby, what are you talking about? Please tell me you're joking, this is some type of prank?"

"Floyd you don't have to play dumb, I know all about you and Alana."

"Alana, what about Alana?"

"Floyd you can quit the act I know you and Alana had an affair behind my back, and she's pregnant with your child."

"Where the fuck did you hear that? That's the craziest shit I've ever heard. I don't even like that bitch. I've been trying to get her out of our lives since the day I met you. I know she don't like me, and the feeling is mutual; but for her to tell you this bald-face lie can only mean her sole intent is to break us up. I don't believe you fell for that shit."

"You're saying you never had sex with Alana?"

"Baby I swear I never touched Alana; let alone had sex with her. I love you more than the air I breathe. I would never do anything I know would hurt you. Baby you know Alana's been jealous of our relationship from day one. If she told you I had sex with her, she straight up lied. Right before I left town I told Alana we were getting married, and it was time for her to let you go and start living her own life."

"You did? Awe Floyd I'm so sorry; you do forgive me, do you?"

"Yes I forgive you, how could I not, I love you. Tell Alana I'm ma deal with her ass when I see her."

"Baby it's alright, I will handle her. Floyd, oh Baby you got to get out of there!" She shouted sending off a series of shock waves.

"What have you done?" I asked, damn near afraid to know the answer.

"Right after I talked to you two Detectives came here looking for you; I told them where you are. Oh, Baby, I'm so sorry."

The mention of the police hit me like a stun gun that sent a bolt of fear throughout my body. My worst nightmare was now my reality. I slammed the phone down and quickly threw on my shoes. Just as I was about to make my move the phone rang. Something told me to answer it.

"Hello," I whispered into the receiver.

"Floyd?" The voice said and paused. "This is Detective Sullivan."

"What can I do for you?" I asked as though this was a social conversation.

"We have a situation here, we have a warrant for your arrest, and we would like you to exit the room with your fingers interlocked behind your neck and back facing the hallway."

"You have a warrant for my arrest, what am I being accused of?" I asked.

"I'm not at liberty to say over the phone. Is there anyone else in the room with you?"

"No I'm alone."

"Are there any weapons in the room?"

"No I'm unarmed."

"Good, good. Well how would you like to proceed?"

"It's not like I have a choice."

"I'm afraid you don't."

"I didn't think so. I will be out shortly."

"I have your word?"

"Yes, you have my word." I hung up the phone and stared in the mirror. For a moment I didn't recognize the image that stared back. Only God knew how tired I was at that moment; they say when it rains it pours, and I must concur. I scanned the room quickly, setting my sight on the smoke detector right above the bed. It was the perfect size with a compartment big enough to secure the keys to the Ford Taurus, where my gun and papers to my new identity were located. The gun alone would have presented a problem, and the passport and new identification would have suggested I was about to run, and in their books, innocent men didn't run.

Just as I promised I emerged from the room and was quickly confronted by four members of SWAT. After following a number of instructions, I was handcuffed and lead downstairs where Detective Sullivan, Ross and a team of law enforcement agents waited for my arrival. It had been years since I last saw Detective Sullivan and Ross, they were the lead detectives in the unsolved homicides of Calvin and Zuberi.

"Thank you," Sullivan said and took custody of me.

"Thanks for what?" I asked baffled by his statement.

"For keeping your word," He said and led me to an unmarked police vehicle. As fate would have it, I got caught slipping, unarmed and trapped inside a room with one way in and one way out. Any aggression on my part would have been tantamount to suicide by a cop.

The authorities had 48 hours to charge me with a crime or let me go. Monica cut me and she cut me deep. My number one priority was to stop the bleeding, access the damage, and figure out a way around this shit. Monica turned out to be a jive ass bitch; one I could no longer trust. There was no forgiving a bitch that played the police. By right what she did was punishable by death; something I would have to strongly consider when the smoke cleared. In the meantime, I needed Alana to retract everything she said to Monica and convince her it was all lies.

Most gangsters waited until they caught a case to lawyer up. Not me, I kept one on retainer all year around.

"Law Office of David Crawford," the familiar voice of his long time receptionist came over the line.

"Betty this is Floyd Anderson, is David in?"

"Yes he is Mr. Anderson, let me connect you."

"Floyd how can I help you?" The ever so cheerful voice of David came over the line.

"David I'm in the San Diego County Jail."

"I'll be over this afternoon."

I hung up the phone and paused for a moment to survey my surrounding. It was a depressing scene, one I could never adjust to. A week ago I was on top of my game, living lavishly with a plan that was destined to lead me to a life of prosperity. Now here I was sitting inside this nasty ass jail fighting a set of circumstances I had no control over. That was a lie; being a realist I couldn't ignore that it was I that brought Akeelah and Monica in my life; two bitches that committed the ultimate acts of betrayal.

The crime game was an ugly business, where the profits never exceeded your losses. Only God knows I suffered some heavy losses, but nothing could compare to the loss of Lil Bull. It wasn't supposed to end like this.

David Crawford wasn't one of the best-dressed lawyers in the legal profession, but he was most definitely one of the sharpest legal minds in the State of California. It was a blessing to find his calendar clear, fresh off a month vacation and ready to get back in the game. David gave me a copy of the affidavit the state relied on to bring me in for questioning, which contained information I already knew; to hold me would require much more, like the murder weapon, a witness, a confession, all of which they had none. The standard of proof in all criminal matters in the State of California went as follows. The Law required Reasonable Suspicion to stop you, Probable Cause to arrest and hold you, and Beyond a Reasonable Doubt to convict you. I was wanted for questioning, which required a lesser stand than a warrant for arrest. I returned from my attorney somewhat concerned by the Substantial Evidence they presented. I had to be extremely careful, I couldn't afford another oversight; I seen gangsters convicted on far less.

Nearly 24-hours had passed since I last spoke with Monica. I tried to imagine was there anything else she could have told them. There was no amount of protection one could utilize in defending himself against a woman that he lived with. She was bound to hear things she wasn't supposed to hear and see shit she wasn't supposed to see. That was a hazard; a risk every gangster took that lived with a woman.

"Hello." She answered after the operator connected us.

"Floyd I'm so glad you called, I was worried to death, where are you?"

I couldn't believe the guile of this bitch, where am I? Where the fuck did she think I was; on vacation, at a country club? I wanted to kill that bitch. "I'm in the San Diego County Jail, waiting to be transferred. Check it out Baby I don't have a lot of time; I need you to listen and do exactly as I tell you. I want you to pack a few things and go up North; the keys are in the safe. Once you get there call David and he'll let you know the next move."

"Baby I'm so sorry; you do believe me, don't you?" I could hear the sorrow in her voice, but it meant nothing. She played herself in the worse way; I could never fuck with a woman that played the police. Her days were numbered, just like it took a moment to bring em in my life; it was a process letting them go.

"Nothing to worry about love, but I need you to get going." They had two days to put it together, establish probable cause to hold me down. They were back in the field, retracing their steps, talking to anybody and everybody they felt might know something. Monica was on her way to Tacoma, Washington by highway. She knew the drill, stay under until I tell her otherwise. The last thing I needed was for law enforcement to get another crack at her. She had shown she couldn't hold her water, what could I expect from a square bitch without a clue.

Unit 1F was a huge holding cage with an open dorm and a dining room that served as a chow hall and recreation room. It was an intake unit designed to give a man a chance to bail out before they sent him upstairs. It was also where they held you until the State officially filed charges. 1F was basically run like any other unit, with two exceptions, we weren't allowed to go outside for recreation, and we weren't allowed to shop at the commissary. Missing a meal was not an option, especially dinner. Waiting for last call was always a gamble; you either got shorted, or you got extras, it was a gamble I always took.

Just as I entered the dining room, I spotted Phil, from Skyline Eastside Piru Gang, strong arm a youngster for his whole dinner tray as he bowed his head to say grace. My immediate reaction was to intervene. I hated a bully, a so-called gangster that preyed on the weak. Feeling my dissatisfaction Phil met and held my stare. I looked at the youngster, and remembered at his age I was a lot smaller, but my heart was much bigger. Win, lose or draw you had to fight. I couldn't fight for a man that wasn't going to fight for himself. I retrieved my tray and noticed this was one time my gamble didn't pay off. It didn't matter; during that brief exchange with Phil, I lost my appetite. On my way to get something to drink, I gave the youngster my tray. The look in his eyes was priceless; it was at that moment I knew I did the right thing.

No sooner than I walked away Phil jacked him for the other tray. The youngster looked at me, and I threw my hands up indicating there was nothing I could do. This simple gesture seemed to feed into Phil's sense of invincibility. As I stood there sipping on a cup of coffee, and sizing Phil up, I concluded he had about thirty pounds on me, and a three inches height and reach advantage. The element of surprise was the most effective tool when confronting a subject much bigger and stronger. I waited for Phil to return to his meal when I slid behind him. My first blow was a power shot under the base of his skull right behind his ear, the blow was decisive and on point. He was at my mercy, and I gave none. What followed was a fury of blows concentrated around his ears, jaw, and temple. The onslaught was quick and brutal, leaving him with his jaw broken in five places, three missing teeth and a broken nose, and a severe concession that require him to be hospitalized for three days. Determined to inflict as much pain as possible I brutalized Phil until the guards arrived. After being tackled and handcuffed I was escorted to a nearby holding cage.

I was standing in the holding cage at the grill gate when they carried Phil away; he got what he was looking for, and the game chose me to give it to him, which was a small price he had to pay for two counts of strong-arm robbery. I received no pleasure punishing Phil, nor did I feel any regrets. The transition from a free society to imprisonment required a change of mindset. The change was automatic; a switch so quick if you blink you'll miss it.

Heads up, one on one, a weapon or not, I was confident in my ability to handle anything or anyone in from of me. There was a new breed of gangster with professional skills concentrated on hand to hand combat. It was a life or death fight beyond barbwire fences; I was a Boss, responsible for sending many to the next life. Never would I allow an off-brand to make a name of me.

The following Tuesday I was up bright and early, today was the day, court call, charge me or release me. I didn't have to wait long for the state to make their move.

"Floyd Anderson." The deputy shouted. I stepped forward, ready to face the music.

"Mr. Anderson I am Deputy Curtis, the State of California request your presence at the Grand Jury. Deputy Owens and I will be escorting you. Once we step inside the courtroom, you will take the first and only seat to the left. You will remain seated until I say otherwise. Do you have any questions?"

"It's all good, let's roll." San Diego Magistrate Court had more tunnels than Alatza. I was surprised to find the courtroom empty when we arrived. We were on standby; they were still out there fighting to the last minutes; searching but not finding enough rope to tie me down. We sat in the courtroom well into the night; finally, at 9:30 pm the phone rung and the order came to release me. They weren't ready, not to say they wasn't trying to get ready. The worse thing about a murder charge it didn't have a statute of limitations, 30 years from now it could come back and haunt you. For the time being a win was a win no matter how it came.

To be continued......

www.ingramcontent.com/pod-product-compliance
Lightning Source LLC
Chambersburg PA
CBHW051119260626
47170CB00005B/1588